ENDLESS

A NOVELLA BY
CHRIS WINTERS

For Jackie
May 2023

 FriesenPress

One Printers Way
Altona, MB R0G 0B0
Canada

www.friesenpress.com

Copyright © 2022 by Chris Winters
First Edition — 2022

All rights reserved.

No part of this publication may be reproduced in any form, or by any means, electronic or mechanical, including photocopying, recording, or any information browsing, storage, or retrieval system, without permission in writing from FriesenPress.

ISBN
978-1-03-913974-9 (Hardcover)
978-1-03-913973-2 (Paperback)
978-1-03-913975-6 (eBook)

1. FICTION, MAGICAL REALISM

Distributed to the trade by The Ingram Book Company

FOR DAD

Acknowledgements:

For those who inspired, supported,
and guided me on this journey. I thank you.

Cheryll Winters, Natasha Rudaya, Anita Webster,
Miranda Winters-Sayle, Debbie Winters, Friesen Press,
Carol Elder, Rueger, Kevin Watson, Cathy Watson, Mario Tcheon,
Melanie Webster Photography, Matthew Hunks, Mariana and Lina.

Prologue

He made the ten-hour drive from Madeira Beach to New Orleans on August 28th, 2005. It was 6 a.m. when he started out, other than a couple of pit-stops for gas and a restroom, he drove straight through. He arrived in New Orleans shortly after 3 p.m. Hurricane Katrina was classified as a Category 5 storm. It was to make landfall within hours. Most of the locals had already evacuated the city or were still in the process of doing so. Nobody was coming in, or at least not anyone with common sense. The wind and rain had been ravaging the coastline relentlessly, destroying homes and flooding the streets. Unfortunately, the worst was still to come, and he knew it.

He drove along the coast on Route 11 not sure what he was looking for. But once he saw it, he knew. There was a fish and chip restaurant with a small motel attached. He saw from a distance a woman struggling in the wind putting plywood over a window. She was preparing for the storm in the eleventh hour. He pulled up to the restaurant and parked. When he got out, the wind just about ripped his door off its hinges. The woman saw him approaching and wondered to herself, "What business would someone have in this weather?"

He yelled to her through the loud wind and rain, asking if he could rent a room as he approached.

"Mister, are you crazy?! This isn't the time for tourists! You need to get away from here as far as possible!"

He approached her and said, "I could say the same to you."

"I'm not going anywhere. This is my place. I need to stay and watch over things."

"I understand, but aren't you concerned for your safety?" he asked curiously.

"I am, but still, I guess I'm stubborn. How about you? Why are you here?"

"I have a few older relatives that are also stubborn. They refused to evacuate, so I decided to come and watch over them. But I need a place to stay. They don't have any extra room. Can I give you a hand with that plywood? That looks difficult in this wind."

"I'll tell you what: if you help me board up the rest of these windows, you can stay for free, but I can't promise safety. You stay at your own risk in this weather."

"Understood. It's a deal. Why did you wait so long to board up the windows?"

"I told you, I'm stubborn, I was hoping the storm was going to weaken."

"Ahhh, I see!" he said loudly as the wind kept whistling. He reached out to shake her hand, "I'm Isaac."

"Maggie," she yelled. "I'll hammer, you hold the plywood!" Together in the wind and rain they boarded up all the windows of the restaurant and motel. There were only eight motel rooms, each with only one window; therefore, it didn't take too long. The wind made it difficult, but they managed.

After they finished up, the two of them went into the restaurant for some refuge from the storm, a coffee, and a bite to eat. They chatted for a while. Maggie gave him a brief history of her business. She had the motel and restaurant for four years. The venue was fresh fish-n-chips and crab in a diner style setting. The restaurant was her pride and joy. She had saved for years to get it up and running and spent every waking minute there.

Maggie eventually showed him to one of the now boarded up rooms, it was modest yet sufficient for his needs.

The next morning, he left early for downtown New Orleans, driving most of the way through six inches of water. Within hours, the flooding would render all cars useless. The damage proved to be devastating for coastline businesses as the flooding reached the whole city. Even historic Bourbon Street was under water. The city was in complete chaos. He had helped as many people as he could, rescuing them from anywhere they found high ground. After two days of driving around in a small motorboat, he and other volunteers had saved dozens of stranded people, but unfortunately, he saw just as many dead and drowned. He had not slept much in those two days, no one did. Once things calmed, he decided to go back to the motel to check on Maggie. He found her as broken as her business itself. She was devastated. She had lost everything: the restaurant and the motel were completely flooded over. She had been waiting on the roof for over a day for help to arrive.

In the weeks following Hurricane Katrina, after Isaac returned home to Florida, he thought about Maggie and her situation a lot. He owned an antique shop in Madeira Beach, with some available space attached. He'd been thinking about selling part of it, but then decided to offer it to her. Maybe she could restart her business in Florida. He had a small apartment above a vacant storefront next to his shop. He called her with the offer. She had been so desperate for good news that she accepted his proposal immediately. She took her insurance settlement money, moved to Florida, and within weeks, she opened the Frittery. That was 14 years ago, and she hasn't looked back since. The Frittery eventually became a local hotspot in Madeira Beach. The business model was fresh seafood, caught daily and made into fritters. It was a slow start at first, but word got out, and her business became popular after only a few months.

During the summer, both the Frittery and the antique shop were a little slower. Florida summer heat tended to scare the tourists away, so Maggie would open only Friday through Sunday during the hot season. Sometimes he'd get her to help in his shop during that slow time. It worked out well for the both of them, she could make some extra money, and he'd have someone to look after the shop while he went on his frequent impromptu trips.

Over the years, Isaac and Maggie became good friends. She noticed things about him though, strange things. He travelled a lot for his work as an antique dealer, and every time he went away, he would return a little depressed. He never talked about these trips, or what it was that upset him, he was a very private man. The oddest thing about him was that he never seemed to show his age. In the 14 years she'd known him, he hadn't changed one bit, not one wrinkle or a single strand of grey hair. They first met when he was 33. Now he was in his late 40's, yet still quite young looking. She came to realize how little she knew of him, which was odd considering she had been his friend for so long, but she respected his privacy, so she never brought it up with him.

1.

It was late on Friday afternoon, and most of the bank staff looked weary after a long work week. They seemed very ready for closing time at 5 p.m. It was a typical warm Florida day, and the Tampa Bay forecast said it was shaping up to be another great weekend. Evidently, the air-conditioning in the building wasn't working so well. He noticed other customers in line seemed a little damp with sweat, as was he. Most of these people were probably looking forward to a nice relaxing weekend. He wished for that too, but he knew it wasn't going to happen, not this weekend anyway. He was at the bank to buy some currency for a trip. First, a two-hour flight to New York in the morning for some business, then he would set off for Barcelona on the red eye.

"May I help you sir?" the teller said, and then she said it again, "Sir?"

Caught daydreaming, he realized he was being beckoned. "Yes. Hi, I'd like to buy some euros."

"Yes of course. How much will you be needing?"

"Five hundred please."

The teller took a moment to calculate the exchange rate on her screen, glancing furtively at him.

Isaac Rojas was an average stature man 5'11", 175 lbs, with brown hair, green eyes, and an olive skin color. He had a slight Middle Eastern look about him, but he could also pass for Italian or Spanish. However, there was one very particular identifying thing about him, he had a five-inch-long scar across his neck. The scar went from below his right ear to his Adam's apple. It was a dull red color but still quite noticeable. The bank teller couldn't help but wonder how he got it.

After a few more exchanges with her, Isaac noticed an older man at the wicket beside him looking over. The teller was going about her business, and the whole time this man had not stopped staring at Isaac.

The older man had heard his voice, a voice that sounded remarkably familiar. At first, he couldn't place it, as it was out of context. But eventually, he realized who he was hearing and seeing, his eyes widened. "Could this be real?!" he thought perplexed. "No, it couldn't possibly be, but wait, the same scar!"

Isaac could see in his peripheral vision, the man looking. It was starting to make him feel uncomfortable. Then the man spoke.

"Cris, Cris Stroud! My God, is that you? How is this possible?!"

Isaac looked at the stranger confused. "I'm sorry sir, I think you're mistaken."

"Cris, it's me George, George Watson! We were in the same division in Cambodia, don't you remember? But you haven't aged a day since I last saw you in '72! How is that even possible?"

"Well, like I said sir, clearly, you're mistaken. My name is Isaac. I wasn't born until 1975, and I've never been to Cambodia." The old man looked confused, yet unconvinced.

"But your voice, and the scar on your neck, they're the same!"

"I'm sorry, George. I'm not this person," he replied sadly.

"So, you never served in Nam between 69 and 72?" he asked suspiciously.

"I wasn't even a glint in my father's eye yet. My folks didn't meet until 1974."

George, scratching his chin in deep thought, said, "Well maybe I'm wrong, but I've not seen such a likeness in all my life."

"George, I wish I was this friend of yours, but obviously I can't be him."

"Well, you never forget someone that takes a bullet for you."

Isaac squirmed a bit at this comment. He knew he'd been made. His ruse was a failed attempt. "Again, I'm sorry." Isaac tried to get back to the business at hand with the teller. She counted his euros and asked if he needed an envelope. "No, thank you! Have a great day." He then turned to face George.

"You have a great day as well George, and again, I'm sorry."

"I guess I'm mistaken. Okay, bye Cris," George said smugly.

Isaac frowned at the sarcasm he heard in George's voice when George intentionally called him by the wrong name again. He turned and walked to the exit, knowing full well that George was watching him the whole way out. George, his old friend, was the last person he expected to see after so many years. As he walked to the door, he thought to himself, "*It's time to relocate, once again.*" He sighed.

Isaac walked to his car as George looked on. George then pulled out his cell phone and made a quick call. After a few rings, a man answered.

"J. Watson Investigations," the voice said.

"Hi, Johnny. Hey, listen, something interesting just popped up, and I need to hire you for a job."

The man replied, "Umm, hey Dad. Since when do you have a job for me?"

"Since now. Something strange just happened, and you're probably going to think I'm nuts. I'll call you later to explain it. Just have an open mind, and do me a favor, take down this license plate number, Florida plate 554WXL, and do a search for me, okay?" His son wrote down the number. George said, "I'll call you tonight." He hung up as he watched Isaac drive away.

George thought to himself, "Am I losing my mind? Was it possible I'm developing dementia? He was at the right age for such an affliction, and the man did look at him in a funny way. But no, you don't forget your best friend who saved your life. You don't forget their voice, and you surely don't forget such a unique scar across their neck. This man is Cris Stroud, and there was no mistaking it! How was it that he looks exactly the same after 47 years though? And why wouldn't he acknowledge me?"

George's son John was a private investigator, and a damn good one at that. He was confident that John would figure out what was happening. To see Cris Stroud again after all these years was unexpected. George knew he would not be alive today if it weren't for this man.

2.

Isaac landed at LaGuardia Airport at 10:15 am Saturday morning. Once he left the terminal, he hailed a cab to go to Sotheby's Auction House on New York's Upper East Side. Traffic wasn't usually too bad at that time on a weekend. He needed to be there by the early afternoon to auction off his Roman broadsword. Flying through airports with a weapon was a bit of a task nowadays, ever since 9/11. He had a bunch of forms to fill out, the sword needed to be packed in a crate, and then he had to check it in with his luggage in Tampa. Having all the proper documentation made it all go smoothly though.

He needed to bring the sword in early for authentication, although he already had papers of provenance from an earlier appraisal. He'd hoped to get $300,000 for the artifact. The sword was dated between 400 and 410 A.D., even though Isaac knew the true year to be 406 A.D. After all, that's when it was presented to him.

He arrived at Sotheby's and met with the curator, Angelica Rossi. She was a petite woman, Italian, very pleasant and professional. He also found her quite attractive. Isaac had had dealings with her several times in the past, as he sold one or two items per year through Sotheby's. Due to their past arrangements, Angelica trusted him. They had even gone out on two dates. They would speak on the phone once or twice a month, usually talking about pieces that came through the auction house, and how much money these items would likely bring in. Both he and Angelica shared a love for antiquities. She was more into Renaissance era and impressionist works, whereas he was partial to Roman and Medieval weaponry. But they still managed to get along despite their different tastes.

They would often flirt a little every time they saw each other. He really wanted to go out with her again but was a bit too shy to ask. She had initiated the first two dates. He figured he would ask her out when he had more time. He was always concerned about having to leave unexpectedly though, which made it exceedingly difficult to make solid plans with her, especially when they lived 1100 miles apart.

Isaac had forwarded the papers of provenance and photos of the broadsword weeks earlier. That way the whole production of auctioning the sword would be prepared for when he arrived. Only the authentication was required.

The sword wasn't your average antique weapon, it was owned by a highly decorated Roman general of the time. It had a large ruby and some gold on the hilt. The blade itself was much shorter than swords of different eras. The blade had been sharpened to a point similar to the precision of a samurai sword. These kinds of unique assets made collectors salivate at the possibility of an acquisition. There was a paper trail in the form of a certificate that showed when the general had given the sword to Isaac. Only Isaac wasn't his name at the time, back then he was known as Darius Caro. The certificate was old and extremely faded, which added to the sword's authenticity. Angelica had wondered how an antique shop owner came across such a rare find. She felt that the sword should be on display in a museum. And she also wondered why an antique dealer would part with such a collectable treasure.

The auction began at 2 p.m., and Isaac stood observing from the back of the room while drinking a coffee. He hadn't had much time to think about what happened at the bank the previous day. Of course, George was correct, they were friends back in Vietnam, best friends. Isaac thought about George often. He missed his old friend. Obviously, George had aged, but he was still the same man. He wasn't as tall as Isaac remembered and was a little heavier. He'd lost most of his hair, which was strange to see because Isaac remembered him with long flowing blonde hair and big sideburns, traits of the early 70's. Isaac wished he could have just embraced George and told him why he left, and why he'd never said goodbye.

Isaac often wondered what became of George, so he was glad to see that the man was still alive and well. He figured George had retired to the Tampa Bay area, as many seniors do. It seemed he would never know because now he would have to move again. That's one of the problems with being unnaturally old while still looking young. You needed to move a lot to stay undetected. He just got detected.

The auction wound down to the last few items, and the Broadsword was next. The bidding quickly reached his reserved price and even surpassed it when a small bidding war ensued. Eventually it sold for $327,000. Isaac was pleasantly surprised. He and Angelica congratulated each other on the sale afterwards.

Soon after the auction ended, Isaac signed the paperwork, said goodbye to his prized possession, and shook hands with the new owner. All the money would be wired to his account in a couple of days, minus the fee for the auction house of course.

Afterwards he and Angelica chatted a bit longer about what was happening in their lives, they promised one another to get together again soon. She mentioned that there were some museums in the Tampa Bay area that she wanted to see. Although the museums in Florida don't even come close to what New York had to offer, she'd been to the MET, the Guggenheim. and the Museum of Natural History dozens of times each. Every time there was a new exhibit, she would get an invite to the opening gala. That was one of the benefits of managing a world-renowned auction house. But she had a desire to see other stuff elsewhere as well.

She told Isaac that she'd like to take a trip soon, a museum trip, and maybe Florida was a possibility. He agreed and was pleasantly surprised when she mentioned that she had two weeks of vacation in August. That was only a few days away. He hadn't taken her offer seriously at first until she mentioned the time off. "I think it would be amazing if you came to visit," Isaac said excitedly. "But right now, I have to get going, I've got a red-eye to Barcelona and still need to get some provisions before my flight."

"Oh, what piece of art are you chasing now?" she asked inquisitively. He told her it was a Spanish dagger that belonged to an explorer from the 16th century. That was a lie.

3.

Isaac sat in the back of a taxi heading to the airport after the auction. He knew it would be a long ride. The traffic was slow now. It was a rainy afternoon with grey skies and very humid. He sat looking at the red light in the intersection, slightly staring but more daydreaming. The red glow of the stoplight reminded him of the ruby embedded in the sword. The broadsword had been presented to him by General Servius, for Bravery by a Citizen in the republic of Rome.

It was the year 406 AD. Darius had been walking to the street market when a small earthquake hit. Now he said small, only because many centuries later he would see the devastation of a large-scale earthquake, one that would be the biggest ever recorded, the Chilean earthquake of 1960. So, by comparison, the one in Rome was small.

That morning, he had had an unstoppable urge to go for a walk. While on his walk, the quake started, and buildings of stone began to collapse all around, buildings that were structurally sound for their era, but not worthy of today's engineering marvels.

One of those buildings was a school. He was close when the collapse occurred, and he immediately shot into action. He knew children would be inside, and he knew some would be dead. Darius was used to seeing people die, women, children, and men of course, but children getting hurt or killed was always the hardest to witness.

He saw tragedy at its worst on a regular basis. This was unfortunately something he became accustomed to over his extended life. He went inside the wrecked structure plunging through the rubble and started helping those he could, pulling out survivors and the dead. There wasn't any particular order, just whoever he got to first in the crumpled mess. It seemed that most of the children that had survived were at the front part of the schoolhouse.

Soon after, other citizens and Roman soldiers came to assist. One of the last children he pulled out was a young boy about nine years old. It didn't go unnoticed that Darius went in many times to save as many as he could, while others just stood there and watched. They couldn't be criticized though. They thought that the building would crush them as well, a worry that Darius didn't have to be concerned with.

In the hours following, the parents of the dead and rescued children began to show up. General Servius was the father of the nine-year-old boy that Darius had rescued. The General had been grateful to him for his bravery. A few days later he arranged a ceremony to honor the dead children, and Darius. The ceremony had a few hundred attendees, and this is when the General presented him with his own decorated broadsword for the deed. He also promised to be of assistance if he should ever need anything, which was an early form of saying that Darius had the key to the city.

When the light changed to green, Isaac snapped out of his reflective memory. It was a sad memory due to all the death, but one he would never forget since he had saved many children. He would miss the sword. It had been with him for more than 1500 years. Unfortunately, auctioning off artifacts was a necessity in his life, as was pawning off smaller, less valuable items. He sold them as a source of income. He had to be able to take off to key locations around the world with little notice, and there was no way to hold onto a regular job under such circumstances. Leaving without warning doesn't bode well with employers. Yet, he still required money to live. Selling these items was how he managed that. The antique shop was perfect cover for his way of life. An antiquities dealer would never be questioned on how he acquired such precious items.

Isaac/Darius had lived in Ancient Rome for over 100 years. Not all in succession, of course, but over a 200-year period. He would stay for 15 or so years, leave for some time, then come back again with a different identity. The Roman population was enormous at that time, and people didn't usually live long lives back then, so it would have been all new faces. Nobody ever noticed he was the same man.

He loved Rome back then. The city was very advanced for its time with Aqueducts, and sophisticated engineering that was ahead of its time. The architecture was also breathtaking for such an early moment in history. No place on Earth thrived like Rome did back then.

Isaac was great at blending in and staying hidden. However, during his prolonged life, there had been a few times when his longevity came under scrutiny, which would just initiate a hasty change in location. One time in England in the 13th century he was accused of practicing witchcraft and was almost sent for execution. Fortunately for him, the accuser was a known drunk, and the brief trial ended in Isaac's favor. "It's not as though the execution would have succeeded anyway." He laughed to himself as he thought about it.

4.

George Watson was not one to spook so easily, nor did he believe in the supernatural. Was he losing his mind? he wondered, or was this just mistaken identity? No, to see someone who saved your life by taking a bullet for you, you would never forget that person. They spent almost three years together in the same outfit. They became close, almost as though they were brothers. He was a radio man, and Cris was a medic. The time they spent together in Vietnam was stressful, but they made the best of it. They had each other's back, and they knew everything there was to know about one another, from first girlfriends to favorite books and movies. George was upset after getting sent home at the end of his last tour and never hearing from his friend again. After seeing him yesterday, it was both a relief and a sore spot. He was happy to see Cris was still alive, yet it was difficult that he denied knowing him. But all these thoughts came secondary to the one thought about how the man hadn't aged.

Saturday morning, and George was waiting for his son to arrive. It was 9 a.m., and while he was sipping his coffee, George was contemplating how he was going to explain to John what he thought to be true. It knew it was going to sound insane. But he also knew that John had an open mind. John had found some information after looking up Isaac's license plate yesterday and was on his way over now to share it with his dad. George wanted an address at the very least but was hoping for much more.

While waiting there on his back patio in the morning Florida sun, George remembered the day that Cris was shot. He should have died. After seeing a Viet-Cong soldier lining up his rifle to shoot George, Cris jumped in front of the bullet and took it in the gut. There was so much blood, they medevacked him out on a chopper within minutes of getting shot. After two long years and three tours together, that was the last time they ever saw each other. But somehow Cris walked out of the hospital in Saigon later that same day and became a deserter. He disappeared forever, until now. George spent the first two years after the war searching for Cris, to no avail.

John Watson pulled his car into the side driveway, parked, and headed for the backyard where he knew his dad would be waiting for him.

"Good morning," he said to his father cheerfully.

"Hey Johnny, would you like some coffee?"

John waved his hand in gesture meaning no thanks. George smiled and eagerly asked,

"What did you find out?"

"Right to the point, huh?"

"Yeah, this is especially important to me. Did you find anything?"

While he was pulling out a lawn chair to sit, John explained, "Well Cris is not Cris. His name is Isaac Rojas." He reached into an envelope and pulled out some papers. "He lives at 13535 Gulf Coast Blvd in Madeira Beach, about 20 minutes away from here. He drives a 2017 Chrysler 300, he's single. He owns an antique shop and lives above it. Oh, and apparently he's only 15-years-old."

George looked puzzled at John's last comment, and asked, "What are you talking about?!"

"There's no paper trail on him before 2005, or at least none that I can see with my limited access. 15 years was all I could go back on this guy, he's a phantom before that."

"Is that all you could find? I need more than this!"

John turned to his dad with a serious look in his eyes, "Dad, what is it with this guy? Why am I looking into him?" John was a conservative man, a little chunky, married, with a young daughter, Penelope. He always wore Hawaiian short-sleeve shirts and cargo shorts in the summer, and a sweater-vest in cooler weather. He lived in St. Petersburg, Florida, just a short trek from where his dad moved after retirement. George and his wife retired to Indian Shores Florida, about a half hour from St. Petersburg. He and his son kept in touch frequently, and George was glad as he got to see his granddaughter quite often.

George stopped what he was doing to think a moment before he answered the question. He had to sell it. "Johnny, I've got something to show you. But first, did you get a printout of his driver's license?"

"I did." John took the photo from the pile of paperwork he had collected over the last 18 hours. He handed over the copy of the driver's license and a few more photos that he had taken of Isaac walking into his antique shop.

"They were clear photos, which was good," George thought, because he could see Cris' neck scar in them.

"I have one, too," George said, removing a folded photo from his shirt pocket and passing it to John. "Take a good look at it but don't unfold it all the way just yet."

John took the photo and looked at it for about 20 seconds. "Ok, it's the same guy, and he served in the military. Was this Desert Storm? The uniform looks wrong, and the photo looks older."

"No, it wasn't Desert Storm!" George interrupted, annoyingly. "Now, unfold it." John opened the photo up to its full size and studied it for a bit fully opened, he now recognized the photo from where it always stood on his parent's mantle. A wave of confusion came over his face, and he started to speak but then stopped. He was bewildered and slowly looked up at his dad.

"What am I seeing? You're clearly much younger here, but Isaac looks the same as he does now in these current photos!"

George nodded his head smugly. "Now you know why you're here. And now you know why this is so important."

Still looking confused, John replied, "For Christ's sake, dad, this is impossible! What are we even talking about here? This is what, 47 years ago? Look at you and how much you've aged in that time."

George gave him a dirty look for that comment and said, "Look, impossible or not, you see what I see, it's clearly him! He looks identical to when I knew him in the war, and if that wasn't proof enough, just look at the scar in the photos! That's undeniable."

"Ok, dad, hold on a sec. I don't want to jump to any crazy conclusions here, I mean, he could have a lookalike son, or maybe he had plastic surgery! After all, you said he was a deserter, probably hiding from the military would explain why he didn't want to acknowledge you in the bank. He doesn't want to be discovered. There isn't a statute of limitations on desertion. He could still be incarcerated for that."

George wanted to yell at his son just then, but he was more reserved. He wanted John on the job, so he needed for him to believe. "A little naive to think plastic surgery could preserve 47 years of life though," he thought crossly.

"How can we get more info on him?" George asked. John didn't know if this was a question or more of a statement.

"Well, I need to follow him, gather a dossier of information, and I need to find out why the paper trail started only fifteen years ago. You should know though that after I pulled his credit card, I saw he purchased a one-way ticket to Barcelona. He leaves tonight. Another notable point is that he travels a lot, and I mean A LOT! He shuts down his shop frequently. I checked with some other store owners in the area, and they said that sometimes he'll be shut down for a few days, and many times over a month. One of the owners was under the impression that our guy searches the world for treasures for his store. Others wonder how he stayed in business, since he's closed so often. We don't know how long he'll be gone for, so this may have to wait until he returns."

George was taking all this information in. He was an impatient man, and he wanted answers sooner than later. A one-way ticket could mean Cris could be gone for weeks, or a month even. George couldn't wait that long.

"Johnny, do you feel like going on a vacation with your old man?"

"What? Where?"

"Barcelona, my treat."

5.

Barcelona was one of the most popular tourist destinations in Spain. Isaac loved spending time there, although this time he was concerned. He knew that something bad was about to happen. His thoughts were a bit selfish. He didn't want to see the devastation of one of his favorite European getaways. He was hoping that whatever pending doom was coming, wouldn't be on a city-wide scale of destruction. He'd know soon enough.

Isaac boarded the plane and took his seat. Many times, he'd been through this, sitting on a plane facing the doom and gloom of what was to come. Would it be a mudslide, a tsunami, or another hurricane maybe? It was always a surprise, but never in a good way.

He had walked the earth for centuries. He believed it was a punishment for a mistake he had made long ago. He had faced death many times, only to cheat it on every occasion. And he'd face it again. Most people looked for ways to prolong life, they fought disease with all their strength and every resource available, they ate healthy, they worked out, but nonetheless the inevitable always came knocking. Not for him though. He longed for death. Not that he wanted to die tomorrow or next week, he just wanted to live a normal life, grow old and one day go to sleep, and never wake up. Dying for him wasn't an option though. The punishment part of living so long was immeasurable. For one, you out-live everyone that you've ever loved, and when you are as old as him, those numbers accumulate to a staggering amount of loss.

The real punishment for him in all this was his destiny. At any given moment, he would get an unstoppable summons to somewhere in the world. When this happened, he had to go to that destination. He wouldn't know what was going to happen when he got there. He just knew it was going to be horrific. He would see human suffering at its worst. Whether it was a man-made disaster, terrorism, or an act of God, he knew there would be death and mayhem. To see this so frequently was a stern punishment, but one that he felt he deserved; therefore, he always gave in to the pull. He wouldn't be able to resist it anyway. He tried many times to ignore it, but when he did, he'd become violently ill. It was as though he would get punished for not following through with his real punishment. This was his life and the way it had been, and always would be, so it seemed.

Over time, he became a healer and then in more modern times a doctor. Every now and then he would go back to school to get a new physician's license under a different name. He would have to go through residency all over again, but it's not like he didn't have the time. He calculated that he'd been to medical school for over forty years of his life since the early 1900's, and that was ok since he was in hospital emergency rooms helping people. It seemed that the busier the hospital, and the more trauma he dealt with, the less he would get summoned to other locations. It was as though his sentencing agent was keeping tabs and making sure he was getting his quota of death and suffering.

The captain's voice came over the speaker saying that they would be taking off soon and to fasten the seatbelts. Isaac was hoping to get some sleep. Usually, sleep didn't come easy in the days preceding an event, but maybe this time he could sleep undisturbed for a while. He sighed and thought, "Here we go again."

6.

Economy class flights weren't always comfortable, and the food was usually mediocre at best. Isaac could afford first class but opted out. Lavish living wasn't important to him. He came from modest beginnings. He was a humble man.

He always enjoyed flying and travelling in general. His favorite mode of transportation was by sea. Boats were not usually in a hurry. They would get to their destination, only a little slower. Most times, he was in a rush to get someplace, a place with an unknown deadline; therefore, flying was his usual mode of transportation.

Back in 1925, he was a passenger on a cargo freighter that he knew was a doomed voyage. That was the first time he'd been summoned to take a sea voyage. The boat set out from Seville, Spain. The destination was Boston. He knew the passage was meant to take a week. He also figured the pending disaster would be at sea.

The ship ran into a squall somewhere in the mid-Atlantic. Some of the crew went overboard and perished from the giant waves that overtook the ship. There were 104 crew members on the boat, some of them hunkered down in the lower levels. This would prove to have been a mistake.

Most of the crew couldn't get up to the higher decks, due to the water intake. The freighter was old, and the steel buckled from the force of the pounding waves. There was a massive breach in port side of the hull. Thousands of gallons of frigid ocean water spewed in every minute, from which escape was futile.

Many people had drowned in the galleys before he could get to them. It was higher up that he was able to rescue some of the people. Once he got them to the upper deck, he tried to get them into the lifeboats. He remembered that he had to push crew members over the side into the water to get them close to the lifeboats. (It's amazing how much strength a human can muster up when adrenaline kicked in.) All in all, he got over twenty people to safety before the ship was lost to the Atlantic. He had no idea how many of the survivors were people that he had helped.

The freezing cold temperatures of the ocean took many lives by hypothermia and some more by drowning. He was one of the last to get into a lifeboat as the ship went down. In total 68 perished that day.

After all this, he still preferred sea travel to air or land. He figured that in airplane crashes, usually there were no survivors. Statistically speaking, automobiles were the worst for survival rate among transportation. Those stats would be drastically different if there were as many planes as cars, he pondered to himself, and then he thought, "These were probably not the best things to be thinking about while on a plane." He rolled his eyes at himself and laughed a bit.

He felt himself dozing off to sleep. There wasn't anyone in the seat beside him, so he pulled down the window shade, unfastened his seatbelt, raised the armrest, and started nodding off for what he hoped would be the remainder of the flight.

7.

Sunday in New York, at Angelica Rossi's condo was dull. There wasn't a rooftop patio, a gym, or a swimming pool. Although she could afford such luxuries, she simply didn't have a lot of leisure time. So why pay extra for amenities that you wouldn't use? Her career was a demanding one; therefore, when it came to her vacation time, she liked to go all out and visit other glamorous places, rather than stay in her condo. But what she really wanted was to spend some time with Isaac.

She found him incredibly attractive. His piercing green eyes were the main draw for her. They carried extensive knowledge behind them. She knew he was an intelligent man. History was his strong suit. She often joked with him that he'd be a great contestant on Jeopardy. He didn't really talk much about himself or his past and seemed to avoid answering personal questions. She knew he was born in the Middle East and raised in many different countries throughout there and Europe, which explained his unique accent. It wasn't a heavy accent, but still noticeable, although she couldn't pinpoint it to a specific language or dialect. She figured that growing up in all these countries would give one a cryptic pronunciation.

Angelica herself was born in Florence, Italy. Her mother was Italian, and her father American. Her family moved to the States when she was five years old; therefore, she didn't have an accent to tie her to an Italian heritage. Her accent was now that of a New Yorker.

Another feature that stood out to her about Isaac was the scar on his neck. It was a light reddish color and quite long. She'd asked him about it once, and his reply was that it was a childhood injury. Angelica sensed that it wasn't a topic to be discussed, so she left it alone. She wondered if it had come from some sort of abuse when he was younger. She could tell that he liked her; thus, why she wasn't nervous to invite herself to spend time with him. She just wasn't sure what he was looking for, if anything at all, and she didn't really know what she wanted either. Her life was consumed by Sotheby's. The job was very demanding; after all, you're dealing with pieces of art worth millions of dollars on a weekly basis. Her role was very satisfying, and she loved it. She got to meet all kinds of people from celebrities to dignitaries and billionaires. It was anything but dull. A couple weeks back she had met one of the Rockefellers. This family had been one of the richest in the world, and they often purchased masterpieces. Although, this was the first time she herself had dealings with them at Sotheby's. She came across many rare artifacts in her tenure at the auction house. Occasionally there would come along a remarkable piece. Isaac's sword was one of them. Never had she seen such an exquisite weapon in perfect condition like this one. But mostly the fact that it came with paperwork of its origin. This was unheard of for something that was 1500 years old. She needed to know more. Angelica majored in world history and minored in archaeology at Columbia University in New York. She initially wanted to work in museums, but over the years and through her contacts, she went a different route. Sotheby's was a dream job; she had no regrets. Angelica was career driven, but also a romantic at heart. What little spare time she had, she used to read romance novels and watching romantic comedies. She wanted more.

Angelica's vacation would start tomorrow. "Two weeks off." She thought, "hmm, what to do?" She took out her cell phone and went through her contacts looking for Isaac's number. He was always interested in her back-stories from Sotheby's, for instance, how sometimes the bidding wouldn't go as planned. Some people would expect much more money for their items, while others would be surprised at how much their art would sell for. She recalled a couple years back a young woman had inherited her parent's home. She had found two paintings in storage that had hung on the walls her whole childhood, and she never knew that they were both Renoirs. She sold them both at

Sotheby's, made a fortune on the sale, and retired to the Bahamas at the age of forty-five. They both loved this story, Isaac especially because he longed for retirement as well.

She took a deep breath and pressed the call button nervously on her phone. "Here goes nothing," she thought. The phone rang.

8.

Going through customs always gave Isaac a bit of a laugh. One question that would always come up was, "What's the purpose of your visit?" How do you answer that? *"Well, I'm here because something really bad is going to happen, and there will most likely be lots of death."* Sarcasm wouldn't go over well with customs officials, so he always told them, "I'm here for business." Loss of life was not something to make jokes about, but unfortunately, he was used to people dying all around him. He always tried to keep an upbeat demeanor about it. Otherwise, he'd be walking around in a constant state of depression. All this death used to be unbearable for him; however, he had developed a shell, he had to if he wanted to be able to rise above to help those in need.

After he passed through customs, he craved an espresso, so he searched for the nearest coffee kiosk. Luckily, there was one close. They're everywhere in Barcelona. While approaching the kiosk, his phone rang. He saw that it was Angelica. He smiled and quickly answered it, "Angelica, what a nice surprise!"

"Hello," she said. "How are you?"

"I'm well. Was there a problem with the money transfer?" he asked nervously.

She thought for a second. "No, not at all. The transfer should be all squared away by Monday morning. The new owner loves his sword."

"Okay, great. Then to what do I owe the pleasure of your call? I wasn't expecting to hear from you so soon."

"Well, I was wondering, when do you return from Spain? I was thinking about taking a flight out to Florida to see you if you're available."

He smiled and thought of her request for a second. "Well, I'm not exactly sure how long I'll be here. I just landed a half hour ago. It could be a couple days or more, I'd like to see you too, of course." Just then he had a thought and stopped short of the coffee line up.

"Angelica, I'm sure that I'll be done in a day or two. I have an idea. Would you meet me in Lisbon? I mean, I didn't have plans to go there, but it just came to me. We can tour some of the local museums and castles. I haven't been to Portugal in ages. What do you think?"

Angelica was elated by the offer. "Oh wow!" she said excitedly. "What a fantastic idea! I would love to go." He laughed. She had such a vibrant, upbeat personality. He admired that. He really enjoyed her company too and thought this would be a great way to get to know her a bit better.

"Okay, give me a day or two to get my stuff done here. Then I'll call you and make arrangements for a hotel and flight plan. How's that sound?"

"Amazing, I'm so excited! I mean, Portugal, wow!" Her smile was from ear to ear.

"I'll call you Tuesday evening with a plan." They said their goodbyes and ended the call. He purchased his espresso, drank it, and then a thought came over him. "I can't get too close to this woman. I can't get those feelings again. It only causes pain later." He stayed away from love as best he could. The last time he had deep feelings for a woman was over fifty years ago. He ended the relationship, and it had crushed both their feelings, but it was the right thing to do. He vowed not to fall in love again after that, and so far, he'd kept his promise.

His infatuation with Angelica was still somewhat new. They'd only been out a couple times, and he liked her. "I guess we'll just have to see what happens," he thought. He was attracted to her look and her personality, she had long flowing brown hair and sparkling green eyes. She reminded him of a former love from long ago.

Thinking about whatever was going to happen in Barcelona, and how long it might go on for, he hoped it wouldn't be too fierce of a situation. He'd have to explain to Angelica why he didn't get the dagger that he was supposed to purchase. He could just say he was out-bid. He brought his empty cup back to the counter and proceeded to leave the airport for his hotel.

9.

After arriving in Barcelona, Isaac checked into his hotel. It was an old building, but with a four-star accommodation rating. The hotel was on a side street around the corner from La Rambla Street, a major tourist attraction. The street was quite long and had a grassed in boulevard area down the middle, full of trees, patios, and gardens. There were street performers, peddlers and markets by day, tourists and locals enjoying themselves on the street by night. This part of the city was known to the locals as Catalonia, an area full of fantastic night clubs, restaurants, and tapas bars that were the best in the world. This city, and especially this street, was always bustling with entertainment.

Another part of La Rambla funnels into a big square named Placa Reial, a popular open area surrounded by more patios, stone buildings, and restaurants. This was where he was headed now, in the late afternoon for some dinner and wine.

He found a nice patio with some comfortable seating. He sat down and waited for the server. European countries took their time with menu service, there was no rush or constant table checks. It was much more laid back than in the U.S. where you usually found your waiter hovering close by. Here, you often needed to chase them down just to pay your bill. When the waiter did finally come, he offered water and the house wine. Isaac ordered a glass of Chardonnay. He sat enjoying the wine while looking over the menu. He figured tapas were in order because that's the food of choice in Spain, and it had been so long since he had tasted the Spanish varieties. Another great Spanish dish was Paella which he hoped to order before he left town as well.

As the waiter was returning to the table to take his order, Isaac saw the man slow down, and then he stopped while looking up toward the sky. There was a rumbling sound, and the waiter tilted his head as if to help him understand what he was seeing. The noise drew the attention of others and got increasingly louder with each second. A bit of a panic ensued in the middle of the square. People were backing away, some were running. The rumbling was now a deafening sound from above and was echoing off the walls of the buildings. Suddenly, a small private jet soared out of the sky rapidly descending and then slammed hard into the center of the square. The echo from the crash was louder than anything Isaac had ever heard. He stood up and ran toward the downed plane, while everyone else was running away from it. He now knew why he'd been beckoned to Barcelona. It was time to go to work.

10.

Tampa International Airport wasn't as big as some airports, but still difficult to navigate. George led the way through the terminal with his son in tow. He moved fast for an older fellow. John figured it was from all those years in Vietnam scouring the jungle that made him a quick walker. That, and the fact that he had been late picking his dad up, which caused them to rush. This was one flight his dad wasn't going to miss.

John had been late getting his dad because he was speaking with one of Isaac's neighbors. He wanted to research Isaac a bit more before following him to Europe. John had pretended to be a land developer, trying to get information about the neighborhood where Isaac's shop was located. There is a fish shack next door to his antique store. It turned out Isaac was the owner of that property as well. The lady that runs the fish shack, Maggie, was a real chatty Cathy. She said how Isaac had been caught with her in Hurricane Katrina when it made landfall in 2005, and how he had stayed around for a few days to help after the storm, and then assisted her to re-settle here in Florida. Isaac put her up and helped her financially to get started. He seemed like a real nice guy.

On the way to the airport, John explained all this to his dad.

"He always was a nice guy. He would have given you the shirt off his back," George said bluntly.

"Well, it seems he's a noble man also, to help her out like that," John said. George already knew this anyway. When you spend time with someone during war, you get to know them very well.

They arrived at the American Airlines boarding gate just in the nick of time and boarded their plane immediately.

George was looking forward to a good nap on the plane. They would arrive on Monday at 1 p.m. Barcelona time. John told his dad that in the last couple hours of the flight, he'd like to go over what information they already had: Isaac's hotel location and what his dad hoped to get from all this. John didn't like to fly by the seat of his pants, he was a planner. He knew that this was important to his dad. He also knew his dad wouldn't be alive if it wasn't for Cris Stroud, which also meant that he would never have been born if Cris hadn't saved his dad that day. In part, John kind of owed Isaac as much as his dad did.

11.

The relentless whine of the engine was piercing to everyone's ears. People were running in all directions, confused, and panicked. A minute earlier, they had been eating, drinking, and enjoying themselves, then, in an instant, their lives had been turned upside down. When the plane hit the ground, there was no explosion. Most likely the pilot knew they were going down and dumped his fuel before impact, a much easier task with a smaller plane, as it had small fuel tanks that would empty quicker. The pilot probably saved some lives in doing so.

Isaac saw the plane hit the ground and bounce once, before skidding and hitting one of the buildings at the far end of the square. The plane itself broke into two sections, almost right at the midpoint of the cabin. Any passengers likely wouldn't have survived, or the pilots since the nose of the plane was the first to hit the back wall. But there would be a lot of pedestrian casualties. There had been a group of people, some standing and some running right where the plane first hit the ground. There would not have been enough time to escape the pending doom. "Most of the dead or injured were going to be those bystanders," he thought.

It took about 45 seconds for him to run to the impact site. When he got there, the devastation was everywhere. How many injured? How many were under the debris? Priority went to the living, and especially those that were screaming. The dead were silent, but the screamers were like a homing beacon to their location. One by one he assessed and moved as many victims away from the wreckage as he could.

The possibility of an explosion or fire was still huge, so he worked fast. About three minutes after Isaac ran in the first time, other people finally started to help him. Possibly, it was because of their adrenalin kicking in, or maybe they saw him going in repeatedly without harm and followed his lead. Whichever the reason, he was glad for the help. People were now approaching him and asking what they could do. He wasn't sure why they came to him, but most likely because he seemed to be the only person who knew what to do.

There were many crushed and broken victims that could not be saved, and those were just the ones he could see. Who knew if anyone was under the fuselage of the plane? He directed people to start checking under debris for survivors.

He noticed a lot of bystanders taking videos and photos with their phones. This was typical nowadays. Some people were more interested in posting on their social media than getting involved. He had no patience for them. He understood that some might be too scared to help, but he couldn't comprehend why they would not give the dignity that the casualties deserved.

While he searched more, he came across a young woman. She looked like she wasn't breathing. He couldn't see any trauma on her body once he approached. He tried to get a pulse but couldn't tell as the rumbling of the jet engine was still so loud. He looked at her chest to see if there was movement, there was not. He frantically started CPR, 30 compressions and two breaths, then repeat. After two repetitions, he anxiously waited for her to recover. She finally gasped desperately for air and started coming around. He then moved her on to her side into the recovery position. When she opened her eyes, he told her she'd be fine. It was then that he noticed a teenager with a cell phone recording him. Isaac hollered at the teen, then jumped up and slapped the phone out of his hand. The young man stepped back startled but apologizing.

Several minutes went by before ambulances and police started to arrive. The plane engine finally came to a stop. The cacophony of sound that it had been emitting was unsettling, and he was glad it had ceased. Some of the police and firefighters were scavenging through the rubble for survivors, while other firemen were spraying foam on the plane to prevent any ignition of flames. He kept searching for more survivors and anyone he could help. Thankfully, it was mostly people with minor injuries now.

He left as soon as things were under control. He knew the press would be on their way. He wanted no part of that. Placa Reial had always been a fond place for him, but now, not so much.

12.

"Hola, puedo hablar con tu enfermera jefe?" Isaac asked, which translated to, "Hello, may I speak to your head nurse?"

He'd learned Spanish a long time ago, and now, at the Hospital De Barcelona, his knowledge of the language would come in handy, although he wasn't completely fluent. The nurse on duty asked him what he needed, stating that she was quite busy. He showed her his medical license and asked if he could be of service. She looked at the card and then back at him sort of puzzled, and he knew why, the date of completion showed 1999. He knew that he looked the same, even though more than 20 years had passed. The nurse didn't have time to pay too much attention to this though, as she had about 40 patients from the plane crash in her E.R.

"Habla Ingles por favor," she said sternly, which meant: "Speak English, please." He figured his broken Spanish must have offended her.

"Yes, you can help, but your credentials are not accepted here without a background check, and we simply don't have the time for that. Please, only help with dressing wounds and assisting the nurses. Do not do any more than they ask of you. Normally, I would say no, but we need all the help we can get. This is nurse Esperanza right here." She explained the situation to the other nurse and handed him off to her.

Isaac didn't stay long at the crash site. He needed to avoid the press and thought he could be of more service at the hospital. After a few hours of assisting, and mostly being a gopher, they were starting to catch up. Wounds were dressed, and patients that needed surgery were in surgery. The chaos seemed to be getting under control.

Doctors from different hospitals had come to help. Some people had died, some were critical, and some walked away with relatively minor injuries. Isaac saw the young woman that he performed CPR on. She seemed alright now. He spoke with her briefly and found out that she had a bunch of broken ribs and a concussion. He figured the broken ribs were from his compressions. They say if you break ribs during CPR, then you've done it correctly. He was happy to see that she was going to be ok. It was by no means the worst disaster he'd seen in his years, but it was still dreadful.

Nurse Esperanza sent him off to the cafeteria for a free meal, with a few handshakes from the triage staff. As he walked away from the emergency room, he passed the waiting room and noticed the teenager that filmed him at the crash site sitting there, still on his phone, but texting this time. Isaac frowned and kept walking.

The television in the cafeteria was showing the footage from the accident. They said nineteen people had died. There were no survivors from inside the plane. Six passengers, two pilots, and eleven pedestrians in the square had perished. Dozens more had been injured from debris and getting thrown. The news was now worldwide.

Just as Isaac was about to devour a tuna fish sandwich, he then saw his own face on the TV screen. It showed him doing CPR, then looking up and yelling at the teen that was holding the very phone that was now displaying his face to the world. It was the same teen he just passed in the waiting room. Isaac sighed and dropped his head as though he'd been defeated in battle. "Perfect end to a perfect day," he thought. He wanted to go and punch the teen in his face for taking videos of people dying, but what good would that do? He should have taken the phone at the time and broke it! He wanted to confront the kid, so he resignedly left his sandwich, got up and went to do just that.

Once he arrived at the waiting room, he sat down beside the teen unnoticed, then he cleared his throat to get the young man's attention. When the teen looked over, he instantly recognized Isaac.

"You're the guy!"

"Yeah, I'm the guy, you stupid ass!"

"Hey, mister, you don't understand. I wasn't being disrespectful; I was filming the whole time. I saw the plane coming and started to record. I didn't realize it was going to crash right there! I kept recording, and then you came and rescued all those people single handedly, it was incredible! You're a hero, and now everyone knows it!"

"I see," said Isaac, with a bit of an angry undertone.

"The police asked if anyone had footage of the crash, so I didn't have a choice but to show them! I didn't show it to the reporters. The police must have."

Isaac shook his head understandingly, patted the kid on the back, and as he got up, he asked, "Why are you here?"

"My sister had some cuts and bruising. She needed stitches, but she's okay. Again, I'm sorry, mister. You are a hero." Isaac departed with a slight wave of his hand and sighed again as he walked away. Getting recognized by George, and then seeing his face on T.V. all in a couple days was not keeping a low profile. Technology was not his friend.

13.

George awoke due to some small turbulence on the flight. He'd fallen asleep with his screen and earphones still on. This was a newer plane; it had all the best media outlets. It showed all the latest movies, and there was a navigation screen called IFE (In Flight Entertainment) that displayed the plane's distance to destination, location, and altitude. It also had CNN World News, news that was broadcasting about a plane crash in Barcelona of all places. As he watched, he thought how unfortunate that so many had perished. There were reporters, police, and firefighters all over the footage, and Cris? Yes, he was looking at Cris Stroud on the screen!

Watching in utter disbelief of the coincidence, he immediately woke John from his nap with a slight elbow to his side.

"What the hell, Dad!"

"Johnny, look, at my screen!"

John was irritated now, but he rubbed the sleep away from his eyes, and then he focused on the screen in front of his father.

He saw a man doing CPR, then getting up and yelling at the videographer. It was Isaac Rojas. The father and son duo glanced at each other with the same astonished look.

George gave one of the earphones to his son, so he could listen as they watched. The headline read, "Private Jet Crashes in Barcelona Square." And underneath, "Unknown Hero Steps Up." Isaac Rojas was now a hero. "This man gets more interesting with every moment that passes," John thought.

Some of the people being interviewed by the reporters were asked about what they saw and did, and whether they knew the man that rescued all the injured people. No one seemed to have been with him or know him. Some did notice that he didn't stay long after he resuscitated a woman. CNN was taking this footage and turning it into a feel-good story in the middle of chaos.

"Dad, what's going on with this guy?"

Not surprisingly, George was wondering the same thing. The Cris hero instincts were evident even back in 1972. George looked at John and said, "I don't know, but we're sure as hell going to find out."

"Let's look at where he's staying," John replied. "We'll be landing in a few hours, and then we have an hour subway ride to the city center. So roughly around 3 p.m., we'll be within walking distance of his hotel. There's a bunch of accommodations in that area. I didn't book anything yet because I didn't know his itinerary. We'll have to wing it from there."

George replied sternly, "No! I want to face the bull head on. We need to get a room where he's staying."

John was shaking his head and speaking softly to try to calm his dad down. "That's a bad idea, we're going spook him, and he'll run."

"That's right, he will!" George hissed. "People make mistakes when they run. Book a room where he's staying!"

John always knew his father to be a direct and hardheaded person, but this man beside him was driven in a way he'd never seen. As he was growing up, he heard the stories about his father's friend, and some of the things they'd been through in Vietnam. John couldn't tell if his father simply missed Isaac and wanted acknowledgement or if he was angry with him for disappearing the way he did, either way, a confrontation coming.

14.

After getting a much-deserved good night's sleep, Isaac had a hot shower and then called the front desk for any messages. The Hotel Catalonia was a quaint place, not like the average large hotel. It was rich with architecture in a building that could easily be over two hundred years old, modernized to equip today's travelers with Wi-Fi and all their technical needs. It was an old meets new establishment.

The concierge told him there were three messages, one from the police and two from the press asking for an interview. He'd expected as much after seeing his face all over the TV. He frowned after reading the messages. Most likely, the staff recognized his face and tipped off the press that the man they were seeking was staying there. He also expected there would be media outside waiting for him. The only message he would return was the one to the police. Better yet, he thought, he would go for a walk to the police headquarters to give his statement in person.

After getting dressed, Isaac asked the concierge if there was a back exit, so that he could leave unnoticed. The clerk pointed the way. Isaac was able to remain incognito in just a ball cap and Ray-Bans as he ducked out the back. Along the way, he decided to call Angelica to let her know that his business in Spain was finished, and that he could meet her in Portugal. He couldn't wait to spend some time in Lisbon. It too was an amazing city. He was also eager to see her again. Leaving Barcelona so soon upset him a bit, but he knew that his face was too well known now, and a quick departure was essential.

His statement was a simple process and only took about a half an hour to give. The police really didn't even need a statement from him.

The only reason they knew of him was the same reason everyone else did, from the teenager's video. Isaac couldn't offer any insight to them as to why the plane crashed. He hadn't witnessed what caused the accident, only the crash itself.

Upon leaving the precinct, he noticed a tapas restaurant across the street. He decided to go in for some lunch. He hadn't had a chance to eat the tapas in Placa Reial because of all the mayhem from the crash.

After his lunch, when he arrived back at his hotel, the foyer was bustling with people checking in. He was able to blend in and hide from the two reporters he saw in the lobby. It was almost 1 p.m. which is the standard check-in time pretty much everywhere in the world, although, he was about to check out and head for the airport. When he walked past the front desk, Isaac did a double take. A man caught his eye. Isaac couldn't believe who he saw. Incredulously, it was his old friend, George Watson. It has been 47 years since he'd seen this man, but now twice in the last 72 hours, on two different continents. No coincidence there. George Watson was following him.

"Damn it!" Isaac thought. Clearly, George was too sharp to have fallen for his ruse in the bank. He obviously knew something was amiss. Even though Isaac was in disguise with a hat and shades, he still turned his head away as he walked quickly past George toward the elevator. Once he reached his room, he wondered how George even knew where he was staying. More so, he was shocked that George had followed him to Europe in the first place! Confused and flustered as he packed his suitcase, Isaac turned on the T.V. All the newscasts were in Spanish, but he did his best to comprehend the fast-speaking reporters. He soon came to realize that all the stations were making him out to be the Hero of Barcelona. "Ugh, time to leave," he muttered under his breath. "If they only knew who I really was," he thought.

15.

"Isaac Rojas, checking out, please," he said to the lady at the hotel desk.

"Yes sir, may I have your American Express card, please?" While looking around for George, he handed her his credit card and the electronic room key. George was nowhere in sight. This time, he needed to exit through the front since that's where all the taxis would be. He finished checking out and walked outside. There were no taxis available just yet, so he stood off to the side and waited with a newspaper. A busy hotel had new arrivals every few minutes. Cabbies knew where to go to make their money.

Right at that moment, Isaac heard a shuffling beside him. "Hi, Cris! So, we meet again, huh?" Isaac heard the voice and knew immediately it was George. He didn't answer or look since Cris was not his name to respond to now. He had to maintain his lie.

"Cris, I'm speaking to you. Won't you answer an old friend?" George moved and was now standing two feet directly in front of him. Isaac had no choice but to respond.

He lowered his newspaper. "I'm sorry, sir. Were you speaking to me? Wait a minute, I remember you. You're that man from the bank in Florida. Wow! What are you doing here?" Isaac gave a fake laugh, even though he was seething inside. "Are you following me?"

"Was it that obvious?" George said sarcastically. He seemed more confident than a few days earlier in the bank, Isaac thought annoyed.

"Mister, I can appreciate that you think I'm someone else, but do you seriously believe I'm your friend from Vietnam? I mean, really?! I don't understand why you're here." However, Isaac knew exactly why George was there. "What do you want from me? I don't know you, I told you this. Now you've followed me across the Atlantic. Are you insane?" Isaac said raising his voice to the older man. Just then, another man walked up to George and stood beside him. There was a familiarity to his face. Then Isaac realized he was looking at the same eyes, these men were related. George had a son, and they had travelled here together. The younger man was a bad dresser, wearing an ugly Hawaiian shirt and cargo shorts, but Isaac could see that he had sharp eyes.

"Cris, would you have a look at this photo?" George asked.

"No. Sir, will you please leave me alone?"

"Indulge me. I've come a long way to show you this."

Isaac sighed as he gave in. He snapped the photo out of his hand and looked at it. The photograph was of George and himself in Vietnam. Isaac remembered it being taken.

"You found a photo of my doppelganger. Congratulations! Please, tell me this isn't why you've flown over 4000 miles? Are you mad? I can tell this is you here, only much, MUCH younger. I mean, I admit I look like this guy, but I would guess he's much greyer and heavier than I am now. He'd have to be in his 70's by now, I imagine."

"Eighty, by my count," George replied smugly. He was a little miffed at the much, MUCH younger comment. He didn't have to say it twice. "Listen, Cris, I know this is you. I know your voice. Your doppelganger wouldn't have the same scar."

Isaac figured there was likely no convincing this man that he wasn't Cris, but he had to stand firm, nevertheless. "I'm sorry, this isn't me. I need to go. My taxi is here, and you're wasting my time with this absurdness."

"Cris, please, or Isaac, or whatever name you go by now, talk to me! You were my friend. What happened to you? Where did you go? How did you leave that hospital in Saigon? Please," he pleaded. "You saved my life, and I never got to thank you."

Isaac now looked at George with a feeling of sadness. He stared at him for a long awkward moment and simply said, "Goodbye, George." He quickly opened the door of the taxi and got in.

George saw something in that look Isaac had given him, something deeper. He'd seen that look before, a long time ago. It was all he needed to know that this was, for sure, his old friend. That look spoke volumes to George. It said, "I'm sorry." George felt Isaac was sorry for leaving, sorry for not saying goodbye, sorry for deserting.

John put his hand on his dad's shoulder and said, "Dad, it's the same man, whether he calls himself Isaac or Cris, it's him." George thought, "Whoever this man became and whatever unnatural ability he had to remain young didn't change the fact that he was human, and a good man." For a brief second, George had his friend back. The man wanted to be left alone, but George was too far into it now. He needed to know the why and how of what was going on.

George instructed John to start tracking his credit card again. His gut told him Cris was going to the airport, either to go home or somewhere else. The man was a hero in Europe. People were looking all over to find him. Social media outlets and news stations couldn't get enough of him. George couldn't help thinking, "For a man that wanted his privacy, he was sure making a spectacle of himself."

16.

The plane was starting to taxi toward the tarmac. It was a midsize Airbus for Vueling Airlines. Isaac was sitting at the very front of the cabin, once again with no other passengers beside him. This meant he could catch another undisturbed nap on the flight.

He'd hoped to get through the terminal unnoticed, and luckily, he did, although the flight attendant that greeted him on the plane did look at him funny, as though she recognized him. "Oh well," he thought, "It is what it is. And he couldn't change it now anyway."

The flight time was approximately two hours and fifteen minutes. Once the plane was done takeoff, the flight attendants would start to serve drinks, and he felt a nice glass or two of red wine was in order after he settled in.

He thought briefly about George, a persistent man, but a good man that simply wanted some answers. Isaac hoped that he wouldn't see him again; however, he suspected that wouldn't be the case. He remembered George was a stubborn bulldog back in the 70's as well.

After takeoff, the plane ascended to an altitude of 10,000 feet, and the seatbelt signs went off. The flight attendants started their service. Since his seat was in the front row, he was the first person to be served.

"A glass of Merlot, please," he said to the flight attendant and went to hand her his credit card.

"Sir, there's no charge for you," she said with a big smile on her face. "All of the crew on this flight are natives of Barcelona, and we know who you are. We just want to thank you, so there's no charge for anything you ask for throughout the flight. We appreciate what you've done!"

He was sure the embarrassment on his face was obvious, as he didn't take compliments well and felt he didn't deserve them. He nodded uneasily and simply said, "Thank you! You're welcome."

While sitting there drinking his wine he hoped that no other flight attendants would come to thank him. Many times, throughout his long life he accepted gratitude and gifts from the families of those whom he rescued. Sometimes rewards and riches were given to him from past events. He would often accept those gifts as they always helped with his living situation, although he always accepted with some guilt.

One of those times was in 1646. He was living in Marseilles, France. There was a daughter of a wealthy shipping merchant that had been kidnapped for a ransom. This was a regular occurrence at the time, done by a local band of pirates. All the citizens knew who the kidnappers were, but all were too afraid to do anything as the pirates were known to retaliate viciously if crossed. This group of pirates were creative. Instead of plundering at sea, they found it was more lucrative and less work to do their shady business on land. Their method of operation was to kidnap the heiress of an aristocrat, or the wife of a noble, someone with the means to pay a healthy ransom. These bandits usually returned the victim after they received their loot, but in most cases, the women had been cruelly mistreated during their imprisonment. Isaac knew of the merchant and his family. They were an upstanding family in the city. The kidnapping angered him. One night, he decided to act and went off to rescue the young lady himself. Everyone knew the pirates took the victims to their ship, which was docked at the shipping port. They had no worries about police or harbor officials as most of them were corrupt or stayed away out of fear.

Isaac had a flintlock pistol and a sword to deal with these men. He would sneak in late. That way, they would all most likely be drunk or asleep, although it was possible some would still be awake to have their way with her. The thought turned his stomach, but if he went in too early, there would be too many to fight.

Shortly after midnight, he started his stealthy mission. Sneaking through the streets, carrying his weapons, he was trying not to be seen as he travelled. Once he arrived at the port, he noticed a couple of the deck hands were asleep by the entrance to the ship's ramp. These were the men who were supposedly keeping watch. Walking right past them quietly up the ramp, he slipped by unnoticed. Once on deck, he looked for a cabin, most likely, they were keeping her below deck. He came to a door with lantern light behind it, he slowly crept In, again unnoticed, so far so good. Sword in hand, he checked a bunch of doors only to find a scattered skeleton crew all asleep in their hammocks. Most of the shipmates were likely at the local tavern drinking themselves into a drunken stupor on mead and wine.

At the end of a hallway, he came to a door that was cracked open. He peered inside only to see a large, grotesque hairy man being very rough with a half nude woman. The woman was whimpering with fear, but obedient, also due to fear. He recognized her as the daughter of the shipping merchant. This man was the leader of the pirates and the man that all the locals feared. Luckily, it was just him.

To rescue the girl without awakening the other men, Isaac would need to be quiet and swift. This meant he had two options, either knock him out quickly or kill him quickly. The choice was easy, he would kill the man. To merely knock him unconscious would give him the opportunity to kidnap others, and it would put this woman and her family at risk again. The pirate would assume the rich merchant had hired people to get his daughter back. No, he had to kill the man, and he had no problem doing it. He had killed before when it was necessary. And it was necessary now. To keep this family and others safe, the man had to die.

Wasting no time, he opened the door and quickly walked up to the man. Just as the pirate turned, Isaac simply thrusted the sword into his bloated gut. There was no sound, no scream and no retaliation, just a swift death as the man fell to the floor.

Isaac then looked at the woman and said, "If you want to live, you need to be very quiet and come with me now." Shocked at what just happened, she grabbed her garment, quickly put it on and took his hand. He asked her if she could swim. She nodded yes.

They went back up on deck, to the starboard side of the ship. To avoid waking the two guards, he decided to go over the railing. He helped her over where she grabbed a rope to climb down. Once in the water, they swam quietly 200 feet to a nearby dock. They had made their escape unnoticed. Now free of any danger as they walked ashore, she asked him who he was. He stated, "Just a friend." The young lady told him her name was Vivienne Devereaux. She then led him frantically through the streets to her father's estate. She had been crying the whole way, probably from relief of her ordeal. She held onto Isaac's arm so tightly that it pinched. Isaac didn't care. He knew she was simply happy to be alive and free once again. Once they arrived at the estate, she started yelling for her father before she even went into the house.

The Devereaux's were still awake. With their daughter in peril, sleep was hard to come by. Upon hearing the front door open and a bunch of yelling and crying, Monsieur and Madame Devereaux came running. The stunned parents were ecstatic at their daughters return. The hugs were heartfelt and long. Her father was so happy to see his daughter that he was in tears. Vivienne pointed to Isaac as her rescuer. Isaac introduced himself, simply by his first name. He explained what happened, that the leader of the Kidnappers was dead, and that there should be no retaliation as it was this leader of the pirates that was feared the most, not his men. The family and Vivienne were extremely grateful to him for what he'd done. The servants brought them towels to dry off with. Mr. Devereaux insisted that Isaac come as their guest of honor for dinner the next evening. He accepted their offer.

That next night, at the end of the feast, Monsieur Devereaux presented Isaac with a box of gold coins and jewels as a reward for his bravery. Isaac had not asked or expected such a gift; however, he accepted it graciously. Monsieur Devereaux said, "It was the least he could do, for returning his daughter home to him.

Some of those jewels were still in Isaac's possession today and worth considerably more. As for the coins, he'd used them long ago as a means to live by.

The wine kept flowing from the flight attendant. She didn't even ask if he wanted more. She just kept filling the glass every time it was empty. Isaac didn't mind. He had a good head for wine, and he was on vacation after all.

He was excited to meet up with Angelica later. He had booked an Airbnb in the heart of Lisbon for their stay.

He felt himself starting to doze off, which was fine by him. He had an hour and a half left before landing in Lisbon.

17.

Upon arriving at Humberto Delgado Airport, he decided to rent a car. He was no stranger to airports and could navigate them with ease. He found the car rental signs to lead him to the lots where they kept all the cars. Moto-port Rentals would be his choice. The clerk wanted his ID, his driver's license, and a credit card. She offered him a few choices: A Fiat 500, an Alfa Romeo, and a Peugeot. He chose the white Fiat 500 Cabriolet convertible. "It would be fun to drive a stick shift through all the winding, cobblestoned hills of Lisbon," he thought.

Lisbon was a beautiful city, rich with ancient architecture, cathedrals, ports, and bridges. The cobblestone sidewalks and roadways were some of the city's best draws. Mosaics were patterned into the walkways all over Portugal. Some of the designs were very intricate, and the blue and white patterns could make you dizzy with vertigo.

Lisbon was also where the explorer Vasco da Gama set off to navigate, discover and map vast areas of India, and other parts of the uncharted world in the late 1400's. Isaac himself had missed an opportunity to sail with the explorer. He declined as he knew they would be at sea for many months at a time, which did not work with his unique situation. Had he known the explorer was going to discover a large portion of the world, maybe, he would have accepted. Missed opportunities were no stranger to someone if they lived long enough. He rolled his eyes, once again, stopped himself from pondering the possibilities of the road not chosen.

"Angelica would love it here," he thought, returning his thoughts to the present. He planned to pick her up at terminal three just after 2 p.m., which meant he had about two hours to kill. He decided to get another espresso to fuel his addiction. Plus, he had had a few more than usual drinks on the plane, thanks to the grateful flight crew, so a strong coffee would do him some good.

18.

Angelica's plane was descending into Lisbon. She was really looking forward to seeing the city. She wondered if her excitement was more about spending time with Isaac though. Romance was something that has eluded her for a long time, mostly due to the demanding hours of her work.

What she knew of him was extraordinarily little, as he was, evidently, a very private man. She knew he disliked all social media, self-admittedly shy, and did not like his picture to be taken. During conversations on their dates, he had told her that he owned a small antique shop on the gulf coast of Florida, and that he loved the hot weather. The extreme heat there reminded him of where he grew up in the Middle East.

Both of their past dates had been for dinner while he was in New York to auction items at Sotheby's. Those two times together were great, but she was looking forward to this trip, which would give them more time outside of dinner to really get to know one another. Among other things, she wanted to know more about that sword. Most of the antiques he'd sold in the past were not big-ticket items, like the recent broadsword. She was impressed when she heard about it. She wasn't aware that he dealt in rare, expensive ancient weapons, or that he had such exquisite taste as a collector. Most antique dealers usually dealt mainly with trinkets, coins, or furniture, and not anything older than a few hundred years. But that sword was something special, and she was eager to know more about it.

Isaac had told her he would pick her up at terminal three, by the taxi stand. "Would he be in a taxi or a rental car?" she wondered. She promised to send him a text when she landed. She took her phone out of airplane mode the second she touched down. "Lisbon was going to be so much fun," she thought contentedly. She could hardly wait.

19.

John Watson had to wait until Isaac purchased a ticket to wherever he was going next. He would find out Isaac's destination from his source back home. The source was a professional hacker, a geeky 24-year-old computer genius. Every time John wanted a credit card purchase tracked, he would pay this kid $300. It was a small price to pay for valuable information. John was glad that Isaac was so dependent on his credit cards. Tracking him was simpler that way, expensive, but simple. Had Isaac known that a private investigator was on to him, he most likely would have switched to cash only.

After John found out it was Portugal, he booked their flight. Right afterwards, his phone rang. The man on the other end was someone he had tried to get hold of back in Florida. Michael Weber was another shop owner and neighbor of Isaac's. John had found out from Maggie, the owner of the Frittery, that Michael and Isaac would sometimes sit at the counter together and shoot the shit over some breakfast or lunch. Mostly they would talk politics and soccer. John had left his business card with Maggie to pass on to Michael, for when she saw him next.

John told Michael he was an old friend trying to reconnect with Isaac. They spoke for about 20 minutes. An interesting point the man on the phone brought up was that he felt Isaac was very unlucky: he'd been through hell a couple times in recent years. Michael told him that Isaac was in the North Tower of the World Trade Centre on 9/11 and narrowly escaped before it collapsed. Then, a bunch of years later, he was in Indonesia when the devastating tsunami hit.

Michael said he remembered thinking that Isaac needed to share these stories, maybe to help him cope with the horrible things he had seen. He felt pity for him to have to endure two such horrible tragedies. John thanked him for returning his call and for the information. Michael said he was sorry he couldn't tell him where Isaac was because he wasn't sure. They only bumped into each other at the restaurant. He didn't even have Isaac's cell number, as their relationship wasn't like that. They were just two men who mostly shared small talk. John thanked him again, and they said goodbye.

Once John was off the phone, he went to look for his dad. He found him eating a croissant in the hotel restaurant. "Dad, there you are! Hey, listen, I just got off the phone with an acquaintance of Isaac's." He immediately had George's attention.

"What'd ya find out? Anything juicy?"

"Well, yeah! This guy is a disaster magnet."

With eyebrows raised, George said, "I'm listening, do tell."

John explained what Michael Weber had told him about Isaac being at 9/11 and the tsunami, and then he reiterated to his dad about what the owner of the fish shack had told him about Isaac and Hurricane Katrina.

"Everywhere he goes, disaster strikes, and now the plane crash. Who the hell has that much bad luck?"

George was equally curious now about the same thing, "Well, he isn't causing them. I mean you may have a case if it were acts of terrorism. But tsunamis and hurricanes, men can't create those kinds of disasters, so what are we talking about?"

"Do you think this means anything, or is it just a coincidence?" John replied.

"For him to have been there for all of them, would be a remote coincidence."

"Agreed," John said. "We need to find the correlation. Anyway, he just landed in Lisbon, and he booked two rooms for four nights there."

"I guess we know where we're off to next then, Lisbon it is!" George said. "Let's get our bags packed. I wonder why he booked two rooms though," he asked confusingly.

20.

While sitting in the parking lot at the airport, waiting on Angelica, Isaac received her text saying she had landed. He quickly drove to terminal three. He figured she would be outside waiting for him, but that wasn't the case. He decided to give it ten minutes before calling her.

While he waited, he reached into his pocket and pulled out a silver coin, an incredibly old coin. He detested the thing and longed to be rid of it, and what it stood for, but he couldn't, ever. In years past, he'd tried giving it to street beggars, or simply tossing it away many times. He recalled throwing it down a sewer grate in Boston, only to have it returned to him as change from a coffee he purchased days later in Florida. Every time the coin reappeared to him either on his nightstand, or in a pocket the following day.

As he looked down at the coin for the millionth time, he couldn't help but admire, albeit grudgingly. The simplistic beauty of the coin was admirable: it was pure silver, with ageing on most of the ridges. The coin wasn't round, it was more of an oval shape. At the time it was minted, presentation was not that important. The significance of the trinket was the bane of his existence. It was a constant reminder of something from long ago, something he wished to forget. But no, he would never be rid of it, nor would he ever forget, they were forever bonded.

21.

Startled by a rapping on the passenger window, Isaac jumped. There he saw Angelica waving and laughing at him at the same time.

He opened the car door and got out. He said, "You scared me."

Nodding her head, she agreed, "I saw that. How are you?"

He smiled as he walked over to give her a hug. He noticed her hair was a little messy but in an attractive way. "I'm great. How was your flight?" Angelica told him that it was long, yet pleasant, but that she was happy to finally be here. She said that she got some sleep and was ready to paint the town red. He laughed. He liked her personality and her sense of humor. He thought of her as a very classy woman.

"I thought you were going to text me to say what car you were in?" she growled.

"Sorry, I totally forgot about that."

She smiled. "That's okay, you weren't hard to miss in this tiny convertible. This car is so small! It's cute though." She knew she wasn't making much sense. She was nervous and excited to see him. She noticed that he looked sexy in his chinos and blue dress shirt. She felt uncomfortable at how she looked after the lengthy flight and was hoping to get a chance to freshen up.

Isaac said, "Lisbon has a lot of narrow streets. This car is the perfect size. You'll see." He put her bag in the back and then chivalrously opened her door.

Her eyes widened and she said, "Why thank you, I didn't mean to startle you. You seemed like you were in a trance looking at a coin."

"Oh, you saw that. Yes, I was daydreaming, I suppose."

"Is that a lucky coin?"

"Well, no, just a family heirloom."

"May I see it?" He reached back into his pocket to fetch it for her. The historian in her immediately recognized the coin as a Roman Drachma.

"Wow, this is old! Really old! Family heirloom, huh? Your family must go way back. I've seen these before in auction. This is centuries old. Do you buy and sell coins at your shop?"

"Not usually, no. And I couldn't part with this one if I tried." He said almost crossly. Catching himself, he quickly smiled and said, "I mean there's too much history behind it."

The way he said it made it seem to her like he didn't want to talk about the coin anymore, so she handed it back to him.

"So, what's the itinerary?"

"Well," he said brightly, "I figured you would want to get to your room for a shower after a long flight. I got us two adjoining rooms, so we'll do that and then go for a walk. Dinner will be later. Nobody eats early in Europe, it's not cool," he laughed, and she smiled warmly. "Later, after we dine, I thought we could go to a section of town called Bairro Alto. That's where everyone goes for the Lisbon nightlife, mostly drinking and dancing, and there's street vendors and performers everywhere, if you like that sort of thing. Tomorrow, I planned for us to go to a beach in the town called Estoril," he continued, "You will like it there. It has beautiful sandy beaches, surrounded by castles, eateries, and shops. We'll take a train there. Then on the way back, we can stop at the launch site for the Portuguese explorer Vasco da Gama's voyage to India." Angelica was excited, as he knew she would be. He had come to know her a little and figured she might be interested in the history of Lisbon. "We can also go to see his tomb at Jeronimo's Monastery if you'd like?"

"Oh yes, please! Let's," she gushed.

"The kicker for the end of the week is, I'd like to take a road trip down to Algarve coastline, to the towns of Albufeira and Vilamoura. We can do some kayaking and sightseeing there." Angelica was elated with it all. It was nice having someone else plan everything. She had read up on the Algarve. It's where the Portuguese go to vacation. It's a three-hour drive from Lisbon down to the coastal towns. The Algarve region was in the southernmost part of Portugal. It was known to be pleasantly hot in the summer, with some of the best beaches in the world. There were also breathtaking rock formations at the shelf where Africa and Portugal were once connected, millions of years ago. She always researched the history of destinations she was about to travel to. She didn't like to go places uneducated.

"Albufeira is a popular tourist destination," Isaac continued, "with hundreds of little shops and restaurants all fixed into a grid of cobblestone streets. If you would like to do some shopping, this is the place."

"Well, I do love shopping." She smiled.

"Of course, you do. You're a female. Doesn't that go without saying?" he teased. Angelica gave him a light slap on the arm for the sarcasm. She enjoyed his playfulness; sometimes he could be too serious. It was nice to see this different side of him.

22.

While driving, he figured it was as good a time as any to explain to her about the plane crash. She would see it on the news soon anyway. He was surprised she hadn't mentioned it yet.

"So, Angelica, I didn't get the dagger that I went to Barcelona for."

"Oh, that's too bad. Did you get outbid?"

"Well, no, I was sidetracked. Did you hear about the plane crash in the Barcelona Square?"

"Yeah, I saw something about it briefly on the news during the flight. Why do you ask?"

"I was there."

"Yes, I knew you were in Barcelona, you told me."

"No, I mean I was at the crash site. I was having dinner in the square when the plane went down."

"Oh my God! Isaac, are you ok? I mean, I see you're not injured, but what happened?" she asked anxiously.

"I was sitting there waiting for my meal, when a small jet crashed where I was. It came out of nowhere, and it was quite bad. A lot of people died; I was able to help some of the survivors though."

"Wow! I'm sorry you had to go through all that. That's unbelievable!"

"Thank you. Anyway, it happened, and I can't change that. I wanted you to know because there was a teenager there, and he filmed the whole thing. So now my face is all over the news, and they're using the word hero." Glancing over at her now while driving, he said, "I was able to help some people, including a young woman that I resuscitated. It was all caught on this kid's video, and now the press is searching for me. But I have no interest in talking to them or being on camera."

Understanding he was a private person, she said, "I get it, but I am proud of you for helping those people. That woman, did she survive?"

"Yeah, I saw her in the hospital afterwards. I'm happy to say she was fine."

"Wow! Isaac, what an amazing story! Again, I'm sorry that happened, I can't imagine. Maybe that coin is lucky because you were able to save some lives. I'm sure you're a hero to that woman."

"Yes, but a lot of people died, too. When I spoke with her after, I didn't tell her it was me that helped her."

She turned forward and thought about what he'd just told her, "I think it's amazing what you did. You are a hero. And I'm glad you're ok. I know you don't like the publicity, but sometimes the world needs a hero."

Angelica couldn't help but think of how much she adored this man, even more now, after his story.

23.

George and John decided to take the night train to Lisbon. It would be a 12-hour ride, and they could get some sleep along the way. It may be a bumpy sleep but sleep just the same. Taking the train was cheaper than flying, too. Since George was flipping the bill for the both of them. He was retired now after all, not that money was an issue though, but he still wanted to keep expenses low.

George had been retired five years. He had owned a successful home security company for 35 years. He sold the business for a handsome profit in 2014. He and his wife Margaret downsized from their four-bedroom house to a luxury condominium on the Gulf of Mexico in Indian Shores. The money he had made from the sale of his company, and from selling their family home put them in a great financial position for retirement.

Thoughts of his retirement brought him back to thinking about Cris. George was thinking about everything they had learned about him so far. He wondered how this man could look half of his actual age and was very curious about why he seemed to keep showing up to places where mayhem soon followed. Was he psychic? Was that even a real thing? There were a lot of people in the world that claimed to be clairvoyant, so maybe it was a possibility. Why then would he go to these places if indeed he was psychic? He would be putting himself at risk. And why didn't he age? That question continued to antagonize George. Does he not die? Maybe there was no risk. George remembered the bullet Cris took for him. His gut all but exploded! He should have died! Yet, later that day, he walked out of the military hospital, with no assistance. There had been a lot of unanswered questions about it, from the doctors, military police, and his commanding officer, all of them asking George if he knew anything. George didn't have any answers for them. He was sure at the time his friend wasn't going to survive the helicopter flight to the hospital. Hearing about his miraculous recovery and desertion was as shocking to George, as it was to everyone else. As they put Cris on to the helicopter, George remembered him pressing an old coin into his hand. He didn't know why he gave it to him, just that it was the last exchange they ever had. The next day, George couldn't find the coin anywhere. He had put it in his pocket, but when he went to get it later, the coin had disappeared. George was no closer to any answers now than he was when this started 47 years earlier. Seeing Cris again flooded his head with a lot of old memories.

Thinking about that time, he couldn't help but reminisce about certain things. He knew Cris to be knowledgeable, especially about anything historical or geographical. George also knew that he'd grown up all over the world and that ... Just then George had a thought: maybe, John could investigate Cris Stroud's past and see if there were any similarities to Isaac's past. Maybe there, they would find a correlation. John had only searched out Isaac Rojas.

John was in a different room on the train, so George texted him the request. John quickly replied that he'd investigate it but not to expect anything as he figured that would be another dead end. Just like the search that abruptly ended fifteen years ago when he searched into Isaac's past.

24.

A loud knocking at George's bunk room door startled him awake. He got up and opened the door to see John standing there with two coffees.

"Johnny, what time is it?"

"6 a.m., and we have to talk." He brusquely shuffled past his dad, sat on the bunk, and handed him a coffee.

"I thought we agreed to meet in the restaurant car at eight. What is it?" John was excited to give his father the information he'd discovered about Cris Stroud. He hadn't expected to find anything, but what he did find was profound.

"Dad, you're a natural investigator. Great idea with looking into Cris' past. I should have thought of it," he said embarrassingly. He continued, "Cris Stroud showed up on the radar back in 1959. There was a train wreck up in the Sierra Nevada Mountains. It was a derailment, and a bunch of people were killed. The newspaper article said it was caused by a small earthquake that hadn't been felt by many people. Evidently though, this quake shifted the tracks enough to cause the train to derail." George glanced around the bunk cabin a little nervously now.

John chuckled to himself and said, "Don't worry, Dad. We're not in Nevada, and they don't get many quakes in this part of Europe." John had had the same concern when he read the newspaper article. It's a little unsettling to read about a train wreck while you're on a train. Looking a little sheepish, George took a breath again.

"Ok, so there was a train derailment. Let me guess, a hero emerged and saved the day?"

"Well, sort of. Only he didn't emerge. He was already there as a passenger on the train. And he shouldn't have survived the crash. The train car he was in had been destroyed. It rolled about 150 feet down the side of a rocky embankment. Anyway, he did walk out of it, and he saved a few people in some of the other cars, too. He managed to get his picture taken in the local paper. Here's a printout of it."

George took the picture and studied it, while shaking his head. All he could say was "Wow!" He was looking at the same man, not one bit younger than he was in the photos from Cambodia in 1971, and no younger looking than now. George was astonished yet again by what he already knew.

"Dad, you were right! Isaac and Cris are the same man, and he doesn't age," John said. "And if my math is correct, this puts Isaac at the very least in his early nineties! He looks pretty damn good for his age, don't you think? I want to get a hold of his Botox technician!"

George took a deep breath and said, "So what we have here is a man that's possibly psychic, and immortal! How is this even possible? I mean, I don't believe in this kind of stuff, yet here it is!" he said as if he knew it to be factual. He stared again at the printout. The photo was black and white. The newspaper article spoke of how 11 people had perished in the wreckage, and where they had been from. The article also mentioned how one of the survivors rescued other passengers from the twisted metal. In the photo Cris was wearing baggy pants, a suit jacket and skinny black tie, the style of that time. "Even his clothes looked in pristine shape, considering what he just went through," George thought. He wanted answers. Was Cris a time traveler? God-like? Or just an anomaly in a world that we as human beings cannot comprehend, or even begin to accept beyond our normal way of reasoning? Yes, he wanted some answers. Cris owed him that much.

25.

Isaac waited in the living area of their hotel suite while Angelica showered and changed. It was 4 p.m., and he was sitting by the window that looked out over the Tagus River while enjoying a cup of coffee. He'd been thinking about Angelica and wondering where this may go. They lived quite a distance from one another, but that was of no real importance. They both loved to travel. If it were to become serious, the distance could become an issue, but he would have a whole different crop of problems at that point, like her questioning why he didn't get older, or why he would go on trips so often, and where did he go? Long term relationships were difficult. He avoided them as best he could. His had become a lonely existence.

Once again, his thoughts drifted to his long past.

When he married his second wife, Audra, in Morocco in 1554, he had had to deal with all these problems. They had been very much in love. He had rescued her from slavery within the Western Kingdom. Slavery had been a part of Northern Africa for many years. It was more about language than race at the time. It was later in the America's that saw the change from white slavers to black slaves.

The first time he saw Audra, she was being beaten on the street by her slaver. Isaac saw her tortured eyes and felt he had to do something. He followed them to their home and scouted the layout of it. Later that night, he snuck back in and searched for the woman. When he found her, he saw there were other women as well. While the owner slept, Isaac woke these women and quietly ushered them out of the home. He got them outside and told them to get away as far as possible and that they were liberated. He grabbed Audra by the hand. He didn't know her name at the time, but she was his reason for going there. Isaac felt the need to go a little further with her rescue. He was going to give her some coins and jewels to escape to a new home, but she wanted to stay with him. Nobody had ever been kind to her. She was scared and didn't want him to leave. He took her to another town, where the slaver would not find her, Isaac stayed with her. During this time, they began to have feelings for one another. Women in Morocco typically were incredibly beautiful, and Audra was no exception. She had long black hair and big dark eyes. He was attracted to her right from the beginning.

The two of them fell in love very quickly. It was her innocence of the world that he adored. She had never been allowed out or taken anywhere during her enslavement; therefore, she was naive about the world. They travelled to many places during their time together, and he showed her many new things. They were together for 22 years before she passed away from an unknown disease at the time, but what Isaac now suspects was cancer, before people knew what cancer was.

He and Audra had a son. Jacob was eighteen when his mother died. He had started to ask his dad questions in his late teens, questions about why his father never looked older. Isaac always replied that his mother had cast a spell on him of a youthful face. Jacob always laughed and would say, "My mother wasn't a witch!" This constant response never satisfied the teen's curiosity, he never got the real answer and eventually stopped asking. The two of them had a close relationship, and Isaac hated lying to him, or leaving him for weeks at a time to deal with one of his cataclysms. He never got over the guilt of that.

Jacob was killed in a fight when he was 24 years old. A thief broke into their home while Isaac was away, Jacob was home alone. He was stabbed in the neck when he tried to stop the thief. Isaac came home to find his son had bled out and died. Even to this day, it made Isaac sad every time he thought of Jacob, and how he died, alone and in pain. Losing a wife to illness was terrible but losing his strong and spirited son in that way was unbearable. Jacob and Audra were forever ingrained in his heart. He doesn't have videos of them, no voice recordings, as such things didn't exist at that time. He just has his memories. And as time passed, he remembered less and less, which was also unbearable.

Sitting by the window in Lisbon, buried in his past, his thoughts drifted, again, from sadness to anger.

Only if he had not been summoned away by his damn curse, Jacob would have lived a rich, full life. Isaac might have been there to fight the man off. Jacob was another victim of his punishment.

26.

Moorish castles, cathedrals, museums, and beaches were what the first few days of their vacation had consisted of. Lisbon was a city rich with history going back as early as the Roman times. It's one of the oldest cities in Western Europe. Isaac enjoyed touring Europe, but especially Portugal and Spain. He was particularly excited that Angelica was with him. He liked sharing his knowledge with her. She seemed extremely interested as well.

The two of them walked to many of the sites and took an Uber to other attractions that were out of walking range. For the last three days of the week, they drove down to the Algarve as planned. There they enjoyed the nightlife of Albufeira until the early hours of the morning and spent their days in the port town of Lagos, with its beautiful sandy beaches and breath-taking cliff formations. There, they kayaked through caves of turquoise waters, swam, sunbathed, and enjoyed each other's company. They held hands often and talked into the night.

During their time together in Portugal, there had been some romance, light flirting over dinners, and slow dancing with their bodies pressed up close, but they both held back on anything more. She felt he wanted to take things slow, which was fine with her. He had booked a suite with two separate bedrooms, which had intrigued her, but didn't surprise. Despite this, Angelica found it difficult to get a read on him. She sensed that he liked her, after all, he did extend the offer to come and meet him in Lisbon, but she couldn't be 100% sure of anything. Isaac didn't offer information about himself easily, she noticed. It seemed she always had to dig a bit to get the tiniest morsels of knowledge.

They had two days left on their vacation before they would head back to their separate cities. "Maybe this evening, she'd make an advance on him!" she thought precociously. She wondered how he'd react to her making the first move. He probably wasn't used to that. Isaac was a man's man, chivalrous and strong, and he liked to be in control. Yet, he was also shy, which she also found attractive. Everything about him was appealing to her. Angelica had not had many relationships in her 35 years. After college, she buried herself into her work. She had had some boyfriends in that time, but nothing of real significance and no one with the maturity level that Isaac brought to the table. She was eager to see where this would go.

27.

There was a quaint little eatery on one of the cobblestoned side streets of Albufeira. They decided to get some dinner there. It was between the apps and the main course that she noticed something about him had changed. He went sort of quiet, and a somber look had taken over the easy expression he had worn most of that day. He looked deep in thought. She asked him if he was alright. He responded that it was just some heartburn, but she thought the look on his face was more one that a person gets when they've just been told some bad news. Isaac excused himself to the men's room.

He splashed water on his face over the restroom sink as if attempting to wash away the latest development. Isaac's interior radar had just gone off. He was being summoned again. He'd have to leave, and soon. An image of Madrid, Spain had popped into his mind. This was where he needed to go. Something bad was about to occur there. "What do I tell Angelica?" he thought. They still had two more days of vacation planned. But what could he do? He could avoid the pull, but then he'd get ill, not something he wanted Angelica to see or be part of, and not to mention the feeling of responsibility he would have for whatever would happen in the city of Madrid if he didn't go. Resignedly, he knew he needed to leave.

Once again, Isaac felt the burden of getting involved with someone, the lies. The reflection in the mirror showed the weariness in his eyes and soul. He needed to make up a story. He dried off his face, put on a cheerful smile, and went back to his seat. Their main courses had arrived. They clinked glasses and wished each other bon appetit. Over dinner, Isaac began his trail of necessary deceit, telling her that he had received a call from the Barcelona police while in the restroom. Apparently, he explained, they were not done with him and needed some more information. There was a big investigation underway by the insurance company for the airline, as well as the European Aviation Safety Agency (E.A.S.A.) were involved now as well. They needed to talk with him in person, he told her, and that it wasn't optional. He quickly added that it would be best if he went alone, heading off any ideas she might have about joining him.

Angelica, who had, in fact, been about to suggest accompanying him, was extremely disappointed by this news, yet she understood. The plane crash had made headlines all over Europe, and he had been the first responder on the ground. There would be lawsuits, and the airline wanted to cover their assets completely. She dealt with enough insurance companies in her job to know the drill. He told her that he needed to leave first thing in the morning, all the time apologizing profusely.

"Of course, I'll leave the rental car for you. I want you to enjoy your last couple days here."

"How will you get to the airport?" she asked, trying, but failing to keep a smile on her face.

"I'll call a taxi."

She was an understanding woman. He'd have to make this up to her.

The disasters didn't usually happen with such frequency. It had only been six days since the Barcelona plane crash. Isaac figured he was safe for a while. It was usually weeks, or sometimes months in between these events. Therefore, he had invited her to Portugal. He assumed there would be a break. He was wrong.

28.

Upon returning to their hotel, he spotted a couple of reporters out front of the courtyard, and they saw him. The courtyard was open to the entrances of the rooms at this one floor hotel. There wasn't any real security to keep them away, no lobby or concierge in this section.

"Mr. Rojas, could we get a statement, please?" one reporter said in a Spanish accent. "The world wants to hear from the Hero of Barcelona."

Turning his head away from the cameras, Isaac grabbed Angelica's arm and sped past the reporters and cameramen.

"Mr. Rojas?" Isaac fumbled with his keys, and then finally they entered the room.

"Wow, you're a celebrity around here," Angelica said, once inside the suite.

"So it seems."

They ignored a couple of knocks from the persistent journalists. He replied under his breath, "Jeez, I'm not even in Spain anymore, and they're hounding me." The knocking stopped after a minute because the reporters got chased away by the deadbeat staff who finally woke up from their communal nap.

Angelica was now even more intrigued, and, quite honestly, turned on more than a little bit by her hero companion. Maybe, this was the time to make her move, she thought to herself. After all, he was leaving in the morning. She decided to go for it. She casually walked up behind him, both sure and unsure of herself at the same time. Isaac was putting his keys on the table when suddenly he felt the space around him was not his own anymore. He turned to find Angelica inches from him, staring into his eyes.

"Oh," he said, and then said no more.

Angelica moved her arms around Isaac's waist and reached up with her mouth to kiss him as his lips descended upon hers, and he passionately grabbed her chin. After moments of heated kissing, they started walking as one, feverishly undressing each other as he guided her toward his bedroom door, and then his bed.

7 a.m. came early, with the alarm buzzing from the side table. Isaac tapped the silence tab and rolled over (for a quick cuddle). Half asleep, Isaac nuzzled his neck into hers. Angelica stretched and then pressed her body close to his. Not wanting to, but knowing he had to, Isaac reluctantly got up, showered, and got dressed. He wished her a good last couple days in Portugal and apologized to her again for having to leave. She was still half asleep, but he hoped she heard him and understood.

Isaac slipped out the door once he saw his taxi arrived. Thankfully, no reporters were there at that time in the morning. Relieved, he stepped into the cab and instructed the driver to head to the airport. During the drive to the airport, he was wondering what was going to happen in Madrid. He felt a little anxious but knew it would pass.

Isaac had a wonderful night with Angelica. They had been very compatible under the sheets. He felt their connection only got stronger after their night of intimacy. Years had passed since he'd been with a woman. He was happy but also very guarded. He didn't feel good about lying to her, like telling her he was off to Barcelona, only to be going to Madrid. He knew this was necessary, but now he needed to be extra careful that no reporters filmed him in Madrid. That brought him to wondering how the reporters had found him at the hotel. How much longer would this go on? (He wasn't a hero!) He knew that eventually another story would take over importance in world news. He only hoped it would be sooner rather than later. But then again, it would probably be taken over by whatever event was drawing him to Madrid, he thought woefully. He wondered if George Watson could have tipped off the press on his whereabouts, and how much longer before George and his son would show their faces again. Soon, he suspected. His thoughts whirled as he rode in the back of the cab.

29.

They watched as Isaac left in the taxi. They were sitting in their rental car across the street from the hotel drinking coffee. "Let's go, Johnny," said George. This wasn't an instruction to follow Isaac. They were going to talk to the woman. They knew from their check on his credit card that he was leaving for Madrid this morning and that he had only booked one ticket, which meant she wasn't going with him. She would be alone in the room; hence, this would be the perfect time to talk to her. George wasn't exactly sure who she was yet, but thanks to John's sleuthing, they knew what room she was in. They knocked on her door, hoping the coffee they brought her would show they were two strangers who come in peace.

Waking to knocking this early annoyed Angelica. "Did he forget something?" she wondered. He wouldn't have taken a room key since he was leaving, so, yes, he must have needed back in and had to knock. Angelica got up slowly to put on her housecoat as she had morning fog. She groggily went to the door and opened it. Once she saw the strangers, she kept the chain lock on. Alarmed now by the two men so early, she said, "Hello, may I help you?"

"Hello ma'am," said George, "we're sorry for the intrusion this early. We were hoping to speak with you about Cris, I mean Isaac Rojas."

They didn't have a camera or a microphone, so she figured they weren't reporters.

"Who are you?" she asked.

The older man said, "I'm an old friend of Isaac's. My name is George Watson, and this is my son John. We've come a long way to speak with you. I have information about the man you know as Isaac Rojas. And we brought coffee." He held up a take-out bag, so she could see it.

She was curious about what these men had to say for two reasons: first, to know more about Isaac would be nice, and second, because of how he had said "The man you know as Isaac Rojas."

"Who else would he be?" she queried.

"Well, Ma'am, that's exactly why we're here. Could we go for a walk and talk? We'll explain."

"Sure, umm, give me about ten minutes, and I'll be out. My name is Angelica, by the way."

"Ok, Angelica, we'll be here."

"May I have my coffee before it gets cold?" George laughed and handed it to her under the chain lock. She shut the door.

"That went better than I thought it would," George said to John as they headed to the patio.

"Dad, she sounded interested the moment you questioned who he was. I think she's already unsure of something."

Racing to get dressed and brush the tangles out of her bed head, she was eager to listen to the father and son duo. She drank down about half the cup of coffee before brushing her teeth.

After ten minutes Angelica emerged from her room looking a little more prepared for the world than she had when she first opened the door. Looking around, she saw the two men sitting at a picnic table on the patio. She approached them.

"Thank you for my coffee. You said you came a long way to see me. How can I help you?"

Standing to greet her, George said, "Well, first, thank you for seeing us, I realize this is strange. As I said, my name is George Watson, and my son John here is a private investigator." John handed her his credentials as George continued, "We live in Florida, and yes, we've come a long way to see you, more so to see Isaac. Well actually, we've been following him." George sat down, while at the same time watching her face for her reaction to this information.

Angelica, looking warily at them, asked, "Why are you following him?" Staring at John, she asked suspiciously, "Who hired you?"

"I did," George said. Angelica looked back at him. "You see, just over a week ago, I was at a bank in my hometown in Florida, where I ran into Isaac. He was an old friend that I haven't seen since I was 33 years old." This statement raised one of her eyebrows.

"May I ask how old you are, George?"

"I turned 80 back in March."

"So, you knew him when he was a toddler? How did you recognize him?" George and John both smiled at each other. "Am I missing something here? What's funny?!" she asked.

John handed his dad the manila envelope with all the photos and information.

Gesturing for Angelica to come closer, George said, "Here, maybe it'll be easier to show you, than tell you. But I will say this, when I saw Isaac in that bank, he looked exactly the same as he did when I saw him last in 1972. He hadn't aged a day."

Angelica, now feeling that she had allowed herself to meet with a couple of lunatics, said, "Okay then," as she slowly started to get up to leave.

George, recognizing he was losing her, said quickly, "Angelica, please, indulge me for two minutes. Just look at this photo."

Hesitant, but intrigued, she stepped closer to the table. George handed her the photo of himself and Cris in Saigon, "Is that your Isaac? Because that same man, with the same voice and scar on his neck, has his arm around me, yes, that's me. That picture was taken in 1971, in Vietnam. You can tell that's me, can't you?" George could feel himself getting a little fired up. He took a few deep breaths to calm down, so he wouldn't scare her away.

Intrigued a little bit more, she studied George well before answering. "I can see that it looks like a younger version of you, yes."

"Good, then we agree," he threw back a quick glance toward John and continued, "his name at the time was Cris Stroud. He was my best friend, and he saved my life by jumping in front of a bullet for me. I assumed he died on the chopper to the hospital. The medics said that sort of wound was fatal, yet he walked out of the military hospital later that same day, and I never saw him again after that, not until last week. That's why I hired my son to help me get to the bottom of this. And let me tell you, we've found out some pretty unbelievable things."

"Ok. You have my attention," as she sat back down at the patio table. "Go on."

"Unless I seem to be senile, or blind," George said, "I know what Cris looked like and sounded like. I also know that scar is quite unique, and if you look at the scar in the photo, it's irrefutably identical to the one he has, wouldn't you say?"

She nodded in agreement.

"Ok, so we agree again. Here's a picture of his current driver's license, the same man again. And here is a photo from the front page of a California newspaper dated August 6th, 1959. Jeez, look who it is!" he said sarcastically.

They let her look at the article about the train derailment without saying anything and watched her face as she studied the photo. The photo was black and white, but clear as day ... was the scar on his neck.

"Confusion would be a good description for the look on your face right now, Angelica." She looked up at George. "What you have here is a man who does not age, and let me guess, you don't believe in that? Well, neither did we, until recently!"

Angelica put her hand up to silence George, "Ok let's assume for a minute that this is Isaac and that for some miraculous reason, he doesn't age. How is that even possible? It sounds ludicrous."

"Angelica, that's why we followed him to Barcelona and now here, to Portugal. That's also why we're following him to Madrid this afternoon, to get some answers."

"He's going back to Barcelona today, not Madrid," she said confused.

John grabbed the envelope and pulled out a receipt from Isaac's credit card. He handed it to her and said, "We have an insider that can get us credit card transactions. He's going to Madrid, and so are we. And we'd like you to come with us."

"You what?" she blurted! "I'm not going to Madrid with you! That's ridiculous. I don't even know you, guys."

"Dad, tell her."

She looked at John, "Tell me what?"

"Oh, there's more! My son here, being the methodical investigator that he is, did some research before we came to Europe. He found out from viable sources that Isaac was in Indonesia when that tsunami hit landfall back in 2004."

"Okay, so?" she said.

"So, we also found out that he was one of the survivors in the World Trade Centre on 9/11. And he was in New Orleans when Hurricane Katrina hit."

John stated, "We don't have proof or photos of those claims, only hearsay, but why would these people make this stuff up?"

George chimed back in, "So, what we have here is a man who seems to be immortal, and who, for some reason, has an addiction to major catastrophes! He's been in a train wreck in 1959, a plane crash last week, the worst terrorist attack on U.S soil, and two of the deadliest natural disasters in the last twenty years! And that's just what we've found out about this week. Who knows how many more events he's been a part of?"

Angelica, after mulling all this over for a moment, said, "John, may I see your credentials again?" He handed her his P.I. license. She then asked, "George, what did you do for a living?"

"I owned a private security company for 35 years."

Angelica nodded slightly and was deep in thought as she closed her eyes and rubbed her temples. "Ok, you, guys don't seem crazy. Your story seems outlandish, but yes, okay, I'll admit you've piqued my curiosity." Opening her eyes and looking at them, she made her decision. "I will go with you to Madrid. I just hope I won't regret this." Angelica had her own reasons for wanting to know more about Isaac, he was too secretive, a little reconnaissance of her own wouldn't hurt.

Relieved, George replied, "Ok, but we need to go now. Our flight is at 11 a.m., and I don't want to miss it, as I suspect something bad is about to happen."

Angelica told them she would need about 30 minutes to shower, pack, and check out. They said they would wait there for her.

As Angelica hurried back to her room, her mind raced with both apprehension and excitement about all the things she had just heard. She felt awkward with agreeing to go with these two strangers, but their story and documents were riveting. The hotel room was booked for two more nights, but, oh well, an adventure had just fallen into her lap, apprehensively and maybe foolishly, she accepted.

30.

At the airport, Isaac found out his plane was going to be delayed for two hours. So, he purchased a coffee, grabbed a seat, and waited in the boarding lounge for his flight. While sipping his coffee and looking out at the runways through the large windows, he found himself once again recalling past events. There were so many to remember. As if it wasn't bad enough to be there when they happened, he constantly had to relive those events through memories and dreams. His thoughts drifted back to one of the worst and longest cataclysms that he had ever faced: The Black Plague of the 14th century.

In 1347, he had been living in Greece when whispers of a pestilence started creeping their way through Europe and Asia. He had been studying theology and philosophy to become a priest at the time, he was already well-educated, as well as being fluent in Latin. This education helped him to get his priesthood quickly. Father Cari Satoris was the ordained alias he was using at that time. He arranged, with the blessing of the church, to go to England to assist with the plague that was ravaging London. He wasn't summoned to go, like all the other times before. It was his choice this time.

All his time on Earth and all his years witnessing death still did not prepare him for what was to come in the next few years. When he arrived in London, it was like nothing he had ever seen before. The church gave him the role of caregiver for the dying. There was about ten percent of the population that were immune to the plague, he claimed to be part of that percentile, so as not to draw suspicion. It was believed that the rat flea was the cause of the disease at the time. Back then, there wasn't a CDC to jump in and find a vaccine. It was the luck of the draw whether you lived or died. In the end, it was figured that between 25 and 50 million people perished from the plague.

By the time he arrived, much of the English population had already been decimated. All he could do was comfort the dying, give last rights, and absolve the dying of their sins. There were no masses held, as those that were healthy didn't want to be near others, for fear of infection. It was said that the disease could pass from touch or breathing the same air as the infected. The terms airborne and cross-contamination had not come into play yet in the 14th century. Doctors did their best, but prayer and social distancing seemed to be the only (real) defense to the plague at the time.

The deaths he saw were horrible, and sickening. The devastation was impossible to deal with. The mere sight of blackened skin from gangrene, along with the smell and blood that came out of every orifice, was hard to take, even for the seasoned healers with strong stomachs. During that time, he often wouldn't be able to sleep at night from seeing women, children, and whole families wiped out almost daily. The bodies couldn't be cleared, burned, or buried fast enough to keep up. Father Satoris had seen 1300 years of death by the time the plague arrived; however, this was different. He'd not seen so many horrible deaths spread out over such a long period of time.

He moved back and forth between London and Britannia for three years before the plague finally broke off. The scale of annihilation would only be later equaled by the number of deaths in all of World War II. (A comparison he found later in history books.)

He often thought about those days 700 years ago. They were the darkest of his extended life. The helplessness of it all was the worst part. He couldn't save anyone, not one. All he could do was to comfort and watch. This was when he felt punished the most. It was at that time in his life that he decided to pursue medicine, so that maybe next time he could do more.

During those few years, he wasn't summoned away, not even once. He figured, with so much suffering, once again, whom or whatever was sending the summons didn't see the need to send him elsewhere for retribution.

31.

Once he was done with whatever event was to happen in Madrid, Isaac decided he would take another week of vacation and go back to his homeland of Israel. He called it home because that was where his first memories were from. He owned a small house on the outskirts of the Judaean Mountains, a modest two-story loft with a yard. Isaac liked to go back to take in his heritage as often as he could, which had been too long this time around, almost two years, and he missed it.

Years ago, he excavated some space under the house and turned it into a vault. This was where he stored his more precious artifacts, things he had collected over the centuries, items of great value and importance. Some were sentimental as well, like the Roman broadsword.

The vault was 30 feet long and 20 feet wide, hidden under the floor with a state-of-the-art keypad and motion sensors. Some of the more valuable items, housed inside its walls, were Roman armor, shields, gold, and jewels. He also had several pieces of medieval weaponry. Other treasures included civil war trinkets, early 1900's baseball cards, French colonial collectables, and some first editions in literature. He learned early on to collect valuables for future sales. Planes and hotels for impromptu travelling were not cheap. He was glad to have his cache. Every time he went back home, he usually grabbed one or two small items to bring back to his Florida shop. The thought of home made him realize he should call Maggie and let her know he'd be away for another week. The antique shop wasn't busy this time of year, but if there were some customers, she would need to look after it in his stead.

Isaac had been on three planes in the last week so far. This flight would be a quick one, and he was glad for that, even though it was delayed. Isaac hoped that whatever was going to happen in Madrid would happen quickly, he wanted to leave swiftly because people in Spain still wanted his story from the plane crash. He felt a little like a fugitive at large.

32.

John was keeping track of Isaac's flight with an app on his smart phone. He knew that Isaac's plane had been delayed, and according to his calculations, they would be at Barajas airport in Madrid around the same time as Isaac's arrival. Luckily, there were many flights to Madrid daily. It was a hot spot destination. John turned the airplane mode off on his phone during their descent. He needed to be able to keep track of Isaac through the app as soon as possible.

Angelica and George were seated beside each other on the flight and seemed to be in some deep conversation. John was seated away from them, in the middle section. After they landed, he'd tell them that they needed to be in disguise since Isaac could be close by. Angelica didn't like that much; she'd already expressed that she was not fond of sneaking around behind Isaac's back. He could tell that she really liked him.

After they landed, John had them purchase baseball caps and told them to put their sunglasses on. They then made their way to where Isaac should be picking up his baggage.

John considered himself quite savvy, with all his spy-tech. He had all the latest gadgets, tracking devices and apps to find or follow someone. Having a hacker on your payroll helped as well. All the cloak and dagger wouldn't have been necessary if he had just brought some of his equipment. A simple GPS button attached to Isaac would have always shown his whereabouts. But that would have caused Isaac problems with the airport metal detectors, so John opted out of using them.

John arrived at the baggage drop first and did some reconnaissance. He figured he'd be the least recognizable of the three of them since he was seen only once by Isaac for a minute during the confrontation out front of the hotel in Barcelona.

As if a gift from God, he saw Isaac standing at the baggage carousel waiting for his luggage. John quickly signaled to the others to hold back. He put his shades on and kept his head down pretending to text. Keeping one eye on his phone and the other on Isaac, he watched as Isaac grabbed his bag from the turn-style and walked off quickly. John noticed a somber look on the man's face as he walked past. This man was troubled about something, or seriously stressed, John thought. That was good, as his attention would be within his own mind and not on any of his pursuers. Under his hat, John watched as he stopped to pick up a newspaper at one kiosk and then what looked like an espresso at another. John thought, "His life seemed normal enough. He did mundane things like the rest of us. He didn't seem immortal, psychic, or exceptional in any way, just a regular guy going about his business like anyone else."

Angelica and George were now walking only a few feet behind John, who was approximately fifty feet behind Isaac. Isaac stopped and took out his phone, to text, or maybe to order an Uber, and then he turned and looked up. Angelica and George stopped in their tracks as Isaac looked right in their direction. They both froze, and that's when it happened.

A massive bang, a deafening blast with a giant fireball, went off right next to Isaac. In a split second, people went flying. Destruction and mayhem were everywhere, with shooting glass, falling debris, and people screaming and running in every direction. George and Angelica were knocked back on their asses by the blast, as was John. With their ears ringing and almost deaf, they were confused and shocked. It took a few seconds for them to realize what happened. A bomb.

Angelica's first thought was how she saw Isaac one second looking at her, and then the next instance, he was blown up. She dropped to her knees and screamed in anguish at what had just happened. Then, suddenly -- POP! POP! POP! POP! And then a few more. At first, she didn't recognize the sound, above the screaming from those that were still alive after the blast. But then, she realized it was gunfire! There was now an active shooter. She couldn't see exactly where it was coming from. The gunfire sounded as though it came from the same area as the blast. The three of them scattered to find cover, as did all the other travelers within the airport terminal. Whoever was shooting had clearly set off a bomb first.

There was a row of vending machines nearby that Angelica hoped would provide cover from the gunfire. That's where the three of them ran. The cacophony of popping sounds coming from the gun was relentless. Clearly, this was a planned attack, possibly terrorists.

People were dropping like flies. Then she saw the lone shooter. He had an automatic assault weapon and was dressed all in black, with a motorcycle helmet on. He was crouched down and looked to be methodically taking aim before each set of shots, this was a shooting gallery, and the people were his targets. When the gunman rose and started to walk in their direction, Angelica started to panic. They had nowhere to run that she could see. The vending machines were right in the middle of a big open area, so they were vulnerable. Angelica looked around for better cover. There were restrooms to the left about forty feet away, which may as well have been a mile in this situation. They would never make it. POP! POP! More gunshots, but they sounded different now. She peeked around the vending machine and saw the man was facing the other way, walking away from them. Relieved, Angelica figured he hadn't seen their hiding spot; otherwise, he might have kept coming. She peered her head out a little further, and as she did, she saw someone sneaking up behind the gunman, and then he started to run toward him. He hit the gunman on the helmet with a fire extinguisher. The shooter stumbled and went down. This same man then grabbed the downed shooter's weapon, turned it, and shot him point blank in the chest. Everything unraveled so fast and was now over just as quickly.

Angelica was so much in shock that it took her a moment to register that it was Isaac who took the automatic weapon and was now standing over the gunman. But she was more shocked to see that Isaac was still alive, and he had just killed the shooter. All around her, people realized what happened, they started to cheer and cry at the same time. She was relieved to see him alive and well, remarkably well for someone that had just been blown up a minute earlier. She looked over at George and John and realized their suspicions about Isaac were correct, this man doesn't die. John reflected to his thought from a minute earlier about Isaac seeming like a regular guy, he couldn't have been more wrong.

Airport security arrived on the scene. Isaac had dropped the gun and moved away, so he wouldn't be mistaken for the shooter. The security guards handcuffed the dead man on the ground. Isaac then looked up in Angelica's direction as if remembering that he may have just seen her right before the blast. Before he could catch a glimpse of her, one of the security guards started talking to him, he quickly shook it off as mistaken identity.

Police, firefighters, and ambulance crews now arrived on the scene. He hoped to escape before the press showed up as usual. Isaac felt confident that any cameras in the area would have been destroyed in the blast. He figured a few people would have seen him kill the shooter and would tell the police; therefore, he would stay and give a full statement. He told one of the officers who he was, and what had happened, and that he would describe everything, only if they kept the press away from him, stating that he was shy.

The police did keep the press away. The scene of the blast was still too dangerous to enter anyway. One of the policemen asked Isaac to come and look at the shooter's face to see if he recognized him. The motorcycle helmet had now been removed, and as Isaac studied the man's face, oddly enough, he did see a familiarity in the man's face but could not place where from. He just told the policeman that he did not know the man. After a short while, some of the officers took Isaac to a security office to get his full statement. As he walked with the police, he wondered again if that woman he had seen in the baseball cap and sunglasses had in fact been Angelica. If so, what was she doing there?

33.

After the attack, the three of them were walking away from the wrecked terminal. Then Angelica stopped suddenly. "I can't leave," she told them. "I have to go to him. I'm sorry, but I thought he died there!"

"HE DID DIE THERE!" George said loudly, then immediately calmed himself and lowered his voice. "Or at least he should have anyway, anyone else would have! You saw what we saw. He was blown away by the bomb. Everyone else within thirty feet of that blast was killed instantly. He was maybe ten feet away. Angelica! There is no logical reason for him to be alive, yet he showed up a minute later without a scratch on him and saved the day!"

"I know," Angelica fretted. "But I still need to go to him. I care for him, and seeing him almost die, well, I just need to see him. Besides, maybe this is a good thing," she reasoned, "I might be able to get some answers. Please, understand, George. I must do this! Let's exchange phone numbers, and I promise to stay in touch."

"Ok," George said reluctantly, but understanding. "Yes, let's swap numbers. Go to him, Angelica, but, please, be careful. Trouble follows that man everywhere he goes. I don't want to see anything bad happen to you."

"I promise, I'll be careful."

"Angelica, good luck but, please, stay in touch," John added. "There is more to this man than we know."

George felt frustrated that she was leaving, but it still sounded like she would cooperate with them, which was a good thing. He thought all of this was a bit too over-whelming for her. Hell, after what they had just been through, it was overwhelming for him. George had seen plenty of people killed in Vietnam, but it's not anything you ever get used to, and he was sure that Angelica had never seen this kind of senseless chaos in her lifetime. "If she spent more time with Isaac, she would definitely see more," he thought to himself.

Angelica went back to the scene of the attack. Due to police presence, she could not get past the barriers that had been set up. She did see Isaac talking with the Spanish police, who, to her, looked more like soldiers, as they were carrying assault rifles. They were leading Isaac to a security office close by. She hoped he wasn't in any trouble for killing the man, someone had to! Isaac didn't see her, so she found an out of the way spot where she could see the security office door and wait. She silently watched the police and paramedics tending to the injured and dead. It was a horrible scene, so much death, she felt sick to her stomach but forced herself to stay put. There were too many questions that she needed answered.

34.

The policeman introduced himself to Isaac as Sergeant Cortez. His English was a bit broken but not too bad. He asked for Isaac's name and address, and other personal information, writing it all down as Isaac told him. He then stated, "You've had a busy week, Mr. Rojas."

"How do you mean?" Isaac asked suspiciously.

"The T.V., your face is on all of them, from the plane crash."

"Ah, I see, you recognized me, that's why I didn't want to see the press. You see, I'm very shy. I've been hiding from them ever since that crash."

Looking at him, Cortez said, "Everybody likes a good hero story, but I understand. I too cherish my privacy. Well, thank you for your service in Barcelona and thank you for today. You've had a very unlucky week. I understand you're probably a bit shaken up by these events; unfortunately, my questions are necessary because you did kill a man. Please, don't misunderstand. We are glad you did, and you're not in trouble at all. However, we must follow procedure."

Isaac nodded, "I understand, ask your questions." He asked Isaac to recount what happened, but Cortez mostly wanted to know about why he was in Madrid and for how long. They also did a criminal record check, which came up clean. The only concern he would have had was if they tried to go back too far into his history, anything more than fifteen years, and he would need to explain why he changed his name. But the policeman didn't question him about that.

Sergeant Cortez took a phone call midway through the statement. He received word of how many had been killed in the attack, five from the blast and another seven from gunshots. There were 24 injured on top of that, two of them critical. He relayed this news to Isaac and said they have yet to identify the shooter or his motive. They speculated what might have caused the man to go on such a murderous rampage. Was it political terrorism? Or maybe the man had a mental health issue. At this point, it was anyone's guess.

After 45 minutes, they finished up, and Cortez led Isaac back out to the terminal. He had arranged for another officer to take him to his hotel. Sergeant Cortez shook his hand and said, "We may need to reach you again for more information."

"That won't be a problem. Call me anytime."

Cortez pointed toward the other officer. Isaac started to walk, when suddenly, Angelica stepped in front of him. He was startled but not surprised, as he thought he had seen her earlier.

No words were spoken. She just wrapped her arms around him. The two embraced for what seemed like an eternity. He knew at that moment that she'd seen what happened. "But how to explain this one?" he wondered. She was shaking, her adrenalin still on high alert. "What are you doing here?" he asked into her hair.

"Can we just get out of here? I'll explain once we leave this place," she said.

"Yes, of course. I assume you saw what happened?"

"Yes, I saw everything," she said as she tearfully pulled away. "I even saw you get blown up by a bomb, and then you were fine! And I saw you kill the gunman." She looked wondering at him.

"Well, I'm ok. I was knocked on my ass hard, but I survived. Then I realized I wouldn't be for much longer if I didn't do something. I saw the shooter was facing the vending machines, so I grabbed a fire extinguisher that was on the floor. I moved around to flank him and waited until he was distracted, then I rapped him on the head," he said while descriptively showing his arms in a swinging motion.

"You seemed very familiar with the gun," she said suspiciously.

"I have experience. Let's get you out of here," he held her hand as they walked past all the chaos from the scene and up to the officer that was waiting, they followed him to his patrol car.

35.

The policeman dropped them off at the hotel. Isaac had booked the room online before his flight. Not expecting this most recent calamity to occur so soon upon his arrival, he had booked the room for two days. Isaac wondered briefly if today's attack was just random and, maybe, there was still a greater event to come. However, he didn't feel the pull anymore, which was always a good sign. Therefore, he assumed that he could cancel the second day booking and leave early for Israel. But what about Angelica? She was still clinging to his arm as they walked to his room. He thought, "There's no way I can leave her alone after what happened today."

Once they entered the room, he asked, "Angelica, I had planned to go home to Israel for another week of vacation before I head back to Florida. Would you like to come with me?"

"Israel? Wow! Really?"

"You know it's where I grew up as a child. And it's always been home to me, sort of. I feel like I need to recharge my batteries after today, and I cannot think of a better place to do that. I can't think of a better person to do that with. I also feel really bad about leaving you this morning."

"Well," she said inquisitively, "I do have another week of vacation still before I need to get back to New York. So, yes, I'd love to. But I have some questions first. And I have a confession to make. You may get angry with me once I tell you," she said sheepishly. He gazed puzzled at her as he regarded her last comment. He knew it was going to be difficult to answer whatever questions she had but being angry with her was not a scenario he had imagined.

"What's on your mind?" he asked hesitantly.

"Okay, well," she started out calmly. "First of all, I just saw a bunch of people killed instantly, people that were not as close to the explosion as you were. Their bodies were mangled and burnt. Yet, here you are, completely unharmed! How do you explain that?" she asked with rising emotion. "And where did you learn to use a gun like that? I mean, you grabbed it as though it was a part of your own body and knew exactly what to do with it."

"Afghanistan," he simply said. "I saw front line action in 2007. I was infantry, and I always had my assault rifle with me. As for the getting blown away part, I can use an example from the war to explain that as well. When an IED goes off, uh, that is, an improvised explosive device, when one goes off, depending on where it's placed, the debris and explosive power will usually shoot out in only one direction. The actual blast can kill anyone within ten feet. But today, the debris shot out in the opposite direction of where I was standing. I got lucky. I was thrown by the blast and knocked dizzy, and I lost my breath for a few seconds, but I was ok. I don't know what else to tell you. Once I was able to focus, I realized there was an assault rifle shooting off rounds. I guess my military training has never left me. I kicked it into high gear and acted on the shooter. I was an Army Ranger. We were trained to act fast and aggressively."

He was looking at her face, hoping she was buying his bullshit as he was making it up on the spot. He saw her nodding as though she believed, so he continued.

"Angelica, I've had to kill a handful of men in my life. Most of the infantry faced insurgents on a regular basis during the war in Afghanistan. I hope you don't think less of me for the way I shot the man, but it had to be done."

"I understand, and no I don't think less of you. You saved mine and many other lives today. Thank you for sharing that with me. It explains a lot." She didn't feel good with all her questions, but she felt as though she didn't know him as well as she thought she had. With a big sigh, she then said, "Here is the part where you may get angry, I followed you here."

"Followed me? Why?"

"Yes, and I wasn't alone."

Realizing what she meant, he asked expectedly, "George Watson?"

"Yes, George, and his private eye son, John. They came to the hotel room this morning just a few minutes after you left for the airport. I'm sorry, I feel horrible, like I've betrayed you. But the story they told me really intrigued me, and it was very convincing."

"What story? Convincing, how? And I'm not angry with you. George seems to be a very persistent and persuasive man," Isaac said appreciatively.

"Convincing in such a way where they have photos of you from long ago. In these photos you look the same, your hair style, body shape, even your scar. At first, I was skeptical of what they were telling me. Then they showed one photo of what seemed to be you again in 1959 on the front page of a newspaper, after a train derailed in Nevada. So, now there was a dated newspaper article with your face. It all seemed like too much of a coincidence."

"Yes, George and his son," he said. "I'm not surprised at all. He's been following me for a week. I didn't want to alarm you."

Isaac hadn't realized that the son was a P.I., which explained a lot. "Now I know how they keep finding me. As a Private Investigator, George's son must be able to track my credit cards."

"Yes, he can. Isaac, they were very persuasive. I don't know if I am just naïve, but I felt I needed to go with them. And there's more."

"More?"

"Yes, he knew there was going to be a tragedy of some sort here in Madrid, and that you were going to be involved somehow."

"Oh, now George can tell the future also? How could he know this?" Isaac was feeling a little uncomfortable now. Finding out about a private investigator on his tail was upsetting enough, but the revelation that they somehow knew why he came to Madrid was even more troubling.

"They spoke with your neighbors in Florida. They found out that you were in New York during 9/11 and Indonesia when the tsunami made landfall."

"So? What does that mean? I had some bad luck while travelling, that's all. I travel a lot; it's bound to happen."

"I'm not finished. Another person that knows you had said you were in New Orleans when Katrina hit. If you put all that together with the train wreck, the plane crash, and, well, now the attack today, George said it best, you're a disaster magnet."

"Well, first, everyone has a doppelganger or two in the world. Second, I'm kind of shy, and I don't really speak with my neighbors all that much to give them this information. I did, however, go to New Orleans to give relief after the hurricane hit. I had friends that lived there, and I couldn't get through to them on the phone, so I drove there. I arrived afterwards," he said sternly.

"I've heard what George thinks of me," he continued although annoyed. "He's all hung up on the crazy notion that I'm an old army buddy of his from Vietnam, which, clearly, I'm not. Vietnam was long before my time. George also thinks in some miraculous way, I don't age. I think he's delusional or in the early stages of dementia. Which do you think is more likely?" Isaac hoped he was convincing.

Angelica, listening to all this, was starting to feel a bit silly now. "But why do you think his son believes?"

"That I don't know. I suppose I can ask him the next time they show up."

"You expect to see them again?"

"Most definitely."

Laughing a bit for the first time since the accident she replied, "Yes they are persistent. So, you're not mad at me? Do you still want me to come to Israel with you?"

"I would love it!"

"There is one more thing though."

"What is it?" he asked, although he felt he already knew.

"Why did you lie to me about going to Barcelona?" she asked sternly.

"Yes, I did lie to you about that. I'm sorry. I had an unexpected and very delicate business matter to take care of here, in Madrid. I can't really talk about it though. Could you give me the benefit of the doubt?"

"Yes, I will." After what they had just been through, she felt she should accept his apology and respect his privacy. "Your business is your own. Just, please, don't lie to me again."

"Again, I'm sorry if I hurt you, Angelica," he reached and pulled her in for a hug that they held for a while.

Isaac now had to figure out how to get to where he needed to go without using his credit cards. Otherwise, he knew he wouldn't be able to shake these two men tracking him.

36.

Angelica was asleep in the bedroom of his suite. It was 11 p.m., but he knew she'd be out for the night. "Normal people weren't used to this kind of a day," he thought. The adrenal gland wreaks havoc on the system, the panic, then shock, and then the fatigue that ensues. Most likely she will sleep in tomorrow as well. His system, on the other hand, barely even registered fear anymore.

He used the time to book their flight, using his debit card instead of his American Express. He hoped that would keep the Watson hound dogs at bay, at least, for a bit anyway. He figured that they knew he had the hotel room for two days, so he was keeping the second day booking, hoping that they'd think he was still in Madrid, while they would've already left for Israel.

Once the flight was booked, he ordered some food from a local eatery that delivered. Paella was his choice, a rice dish consisting of clams, shrimp, and sausage. He'd really been looking forward to having some in a nice restaurant but take out would have to suffice since he was cutting his time short in Spain. While waiting for the food, he thought again about George and his son, how they had been one step behind him the whole way and getting wiser by the day, how they knew so much, and how all that Angelica said had been true. He had been at all those disasters. Angelica was also starting to get wiser.

"Why did he let his photo get taken after the train derailment back in 1959?" he thought angrily.

The Watson's were a problem, and obviously, they were not going away, which meant he knew (all too well) that once he got back home, he'd have to change his identity and move somewhere else again.

"What a pain in the ass!" he thought. He really loved his Florida set-up. He would also have to speak with Maggie when he got home to let her know not to give out too much information about him when people came asking questions. What would he do about Maggie? She was his good friend. There was no way she'd accept him moving away without a proper explanation. Of all the lives he had created for himself, the one in Florida was his favorite. George and his meddling son had to go and wreck everything!

What about Angelica? He really cared for her. Could he just up and leave her high and dry?

Frowning to himself at these thoughts, he took out his coin and stared at it again. Why could he not have seen how things were? It was one mistake, but it became a debt that continuously collects.

37.

They were at a small hotel in Madrid the night of the explosion. They had a few bumps and bruises after being thrown from the blast. After a brief rest, John started searching online again. "Dad, I got hit on a new flight for our friend, and he has company."

George looked over, "Angelica's with him?"

"Yup, and they're flying to Israel. He's on to us though. He used his debit card on this last transaction. She must have told him we're tracking his credit card."

"Wow! Israel, this trip is getting expensive."

"Yes, it is, and that's why I'm going to cover the cost of this phase of our trip. We'll call it a family discount."

"Nonsense! I was just stating the obvious. This was my plan, and I hired you."

"Dad, I'm into this as deeply as you. I too want answers. It's not every day that you come across a situation like this. Hell, you never come across a situation like this!" he laughed.

"No, no, you don't," George chuckled. "So, when do they fly out?"

"Their plane leaves in two hours, but there's no hotel booked on his AMEX. I even ran a search on Angelica's credit cards, and nothing."

"So, we know where they're going, but not where they're staying?" George asked.

"Correct. I wonder if he would be staying with a friend, maybe?"

"Good thing you're a great investigator," he winked. "All right, we'd better get a move on. I wonder what'll happen next, a murderous sandstorm, a zombie apocalypse or the parting of the Red Sea." Even though he joked, George was a bit nervous. After all, they had put themselves in harm's way once already while following this man.

"Dad, what if we're wrong about all of this? I mean, what if he's just a normal guy with some serious bad luck, and we're over-thinking it?"

"Well, if that were the case, then we should probably be committed. Listen, Johnny, he was my best friend for almost three years! I know his voice, his mannerisms, even his quirks. There are too many similarities. Sure, 47 years have passed, but all these memories came flooding back to me after I saw him again. Three years of looking at that scar in Nam, I remembered every detail of it. He is Cris Stroud! If I end up being wrong, well, then you have my permission to put me in the looney bin, okay?"

"Okay, Dad, I'm just questioning if we're doing the right thing. I'm with you all the way on this, but I just want to be sure. Some confirmation would be nice, some proof, you know?"

"That's exactly what we're searching for, proof. Now let's go find some!"

38.

The next morning, after arriving at Ben Gurion Airport in Israel, they waited for a taxi outside the terminal. Isaac took a deep breath. The smell of the Israeli air reminded him that he was home. It was the smell of dry sand and humidity. Not a great smell, he admitted, but it was an instant reminder of his past, so he loved it. The sun was shining brightly, and the heat was scorching. He had a brief thought of the long garments that he wore back when he lived here so long ago. Some people do still wear them now, as it is tradition; however, it was so hot under the heavy apparel. He opted for khaki shorts and a short sleeve dress shirt nowadays. He felt and looked like a tourist though.

It was a 40-minute ride to his home, in the Judean Mountains. His house was modest and somewhat secluded, with a gate 30 feet from the front door. This house was different from American style homes. It was more of a rectangle with tan stucco, medium size and plain looking. There were only a few windows at the front and back, with shutters to keep the sun out. There was a bit of green space, with some cactus and a few wild indigenous palms.

They arrived at his home where Isaac paid the taxi driver and then unlocked the gate. "Wow, this is really beautiful, with all these mountains!" Angelica said.

"Oh, just you wait until we go for a hike in those mountains. There are structures and rock formations as old as time itself up there. It's quite breath-taking."

Excited by the prospect of seeing the sites, as well as spending time with him in his native environment, Angelica was filled with enthusiasm.

"I can hardly wait," she blurted out.

He was glad she was happy to be here, but more importantly, he was glad she was ok after yesterday's event. She seemed to recover from the shock of it quickly. Isaac liked her company and was thrilled to be able to show her around his home. He had never brought a woman, or dare he say girlfriend, here before.

When they entered, there was a bit of a musty odor. That was to be expected, no one had been there in six months, not since the last time he had arranged for a cleaning service to come in. "There would be some dusting needed," he thought. The house was open concept on the main floor. A large room filled with some rustic antique furniture and a giant expensive Persian carpet, under a large carved wood dining table. In the corner, there was a spiral staircase to the second floor, and in another corner was the kitchen. It too was open concept with a granite island counter but not many cupboards. He told her that there was a bedroom and a washroom upstairs. He apologized that there wasn't any air conditioning, just ceiling fans.

As Angelica headed for the stairs to the bedroom, she looked at him with a smile. She was going to have a shower, and Isaac decided to clean up a bit to make the place smell and look better. He plugged the fridge in and cracked some windows. He would go out the next morning for some groceries and toiletries, as they only had minimal provisions at the moment. Dinner this evening would have to be at a restaurant.

Once he heard her in the shower upstairs, he quickly went over to the dining table, grabbed onto a corner, pushed the heavy table off to the side, and rolled up the carpet. Under the carpet was a patch of floor that had been cut away. Isaac lifted that portion to reveal a steel door with a keypad. He paused for a moment and listened for Angelica again. When he was sure she was still in the shower, he continued.

He punched in the code for the door and lifted it as it made a creaky sound. The door opening activated the motion sensor lights. He stepped in and went down the metal ladder to a well-lit room that resembled a bank vault. He took a quick glance at his inventory of precious belongings. The cache was impressive beyond words, he knew. On the furthest side of the room were shelves of books that were as old as he was. There were first editions, Bibles, and religious scrolls from centuries past. He quickly checked a small cabinet in the back, where he kept some of his more precious things, items that would stay with him forever, some with great memories. After confirming that all was where it should be and that nobody had tampered with anything, he exited the vault, closed the hatch door, and put the carpet and table back in place.

Once he was confident everything was in order, Isaac went about his cleaning. He thought about the items in the room. They were his life's collection, a compilation to live off. The last item he had removed was the Roman broadsword that Angelica had sold at Sotheby's. The sword was one of his favorites, but it was a means to an end. Some of the other items in the vault, he would never part with, due to deeper sentimentality.

Most of collectables were priceless, and he'd done his best to protect them. Twenty years ago, he dug the hole under the floor himself and used just wooden beams to brace the walls. Fifteen years later, he decided to make it more structurally sound and secure, by using steel and adding lights and a security system. When his neighbors asked him about what he'd been building, he just told them that he was working on the foundation and doing some renovations. Nobody needed to know of the vault's existence.

39.

After a long steamy shower, Angelica was getting dressed when her cell phone rang. She looked at the screen and saw it was George. She contemplated for a few seconds whether to answer it or not. She answered, "Hi George."

"Hi, Angelica. How are you? Am I calling at a bad time? Is Isaac near you?"

"No, it's ok. He's downstairs, I have to say though," she lowered her voice, "I don't like being sneaky like this. He doesn't deserve it. He's a good man, and it feels wrong."

"Oh, I know he's a good man. He's a great man. He was my best friend, remember? And he's a hero. Listen, I don't want you to feel sneaky. I just wanted to make sure that you were okay. That was a bad thing that happened yesterday, and we're all lucky to be alive."

"Yes, we are. It could have been bad for us. We were extremely lucky."

"I also wanted to let you know that I'm aware he talked his way out of it with you. I mean he probably made you think it was just luck or something that he survived, and most likely he's making me out to be a crazy person."

"Well, yes, he did say something along those lines about luck. However, he didn't say much about you at all. I know you're not crazy. There were just a bunch of coincidentally weird things going on, enough to make someone wonder about him."

"Wonder, are you saying that you think these are all just random coincidences? Angelica, you're a smart woman, and you saw what happened! I've seen many men blown to pieces in the war, by smaller bombs than that. There's no way in hell a man could have survived that blast from as close as he was. It wasn't a land mine or a pipe bomb. This was a C-4 explosive device. That's what they're reporting on the news."

"But these bombs are directional with their blasts, are they not?"

"Um, no. Why would you say that? Did he tell you that?"

"Yes, he did."

"I see. Well, no, they aren't directional. And besides, he was a medic. He's not an expert on explosives. He's deflecting, Angelica."

"Hmmm, ok, well, let's say for a second that's the case, and he should have died, then what are you really saying here, George? Do you really think that there are such miraculous things as people that can't die and don't age? I think there must be some more logical explanation. Honestly, I'm not sure why I bought into this whole thing in the first place."

He knew at that moment that he'd lost her as an ally, so he gave in. "Angelica, I won't keep you any longer. I needed to check on you. I'm glad you're okay. You have my number if anything should happen. Enjoy the rest of your vacation in Israel."

"Thank you, George," she sighed, "I'll call you soon. Goodbye."

She hung up her cell phone and thought, "Damn, that John is a good investigator. George and John knew exactly where they were." Had Isaac lied about the bomb? She had heard about C-4 before and knew it was bad stuff. A directional blast did seem kind of odd, now that she thought about it more. Isaac had been through enough though. She wasn't going to question him anymore on the topic.

She mentally shook it off, put her cell phone down and finished getting ready. She knew it was trivial. Her next thought was that she just hoped the Watsons wouldn't show up tonight to wreck their evening. She knew they were coming at some point though. George didn't say it, but yeah, she knew.

40.

They had a wonderful time in town that evening. Isaac brought her to one of the city's best restaurants. Afterwards they walked around until dark looking at some of the architecture. He promised to take her to some of the religious sites over the next few days. She asked if he could show her the Dead Sea as well. He agreed and was excited to show her all the places. She had a sense that he loved being in his homeland. There was a noticeable change in his mood. He seemed happier than she'd seen him this whole trip, despite the tragedy. "Going home was good for the soul," she thought.

Once back at the house, they relaxed on the sofa and chatted over a glass of wine. He may not have any food in the fridge, but he always had a reserve of fine wines. They cuddled on the sofa and talked about simple things, both being careful to avoid topics that would spoil the evening, like airport explosions and the natural lifespan of men.

Angelica snuggled in close to him, with plans of taking him to bed again. He was a gentleman and not too quick to make the first move, which was fine with her, she didn't mind initiating. He accepted her offer without hesitation, and after a few minutes of passion on the sofa, he took her hand and led her up the spiral staircase. "I'm beginning to really like this woman," he thought wryly. Still, getting close was always a problem. He was conflicted on how far to take it with her, but he would worry about that later. Right now, he couldn't think of anything except how her skin smelled and how her hair felt to the touch. Within minutes, they took the spiral staircase to the bedroom.

The next morning, he told her he needed to go to the market for groceries and then some banking that he had to take care of. He said he had a few investments here that he wanted to check on after a two-year absence. He'd only be away a few hours. She replied sleepily, "Sure. And thank you for last night. I had a wonderful time." He raised an eyebrow, and she smiled and winked.

There was a dress shop that they'd passed on their walk home last night. She had seen some nice things in the window, and she told him she was going to walk back there to try some of them on. He asked if she wanted him to join her. "No, you go do your banking. I'll be fine. It's only ten minutes away. Thank you though, you're sweet."

He smiled and said, "I'll see you soon. Enjoy your shopping."

After he left, Angelica hopped out of the bed. She was looking forward to shopping at the boutique. There was specifically a full-length gown that she'd seen and admired in the window the night before. Once she was dressed and ready, she locked up using the key Isaac left her and started her walk.

41.

Isaac wanted to make a stop before he went to the market. He instructed his taxi driver to take him to Golgotha, a place best known for the crucifixion. He had not visited the site for quite some time. That had been a dreadful point in history, perhaps, one of the worst. Isaac can only think of a few other times that had the same type of notoriety, both World Wars and the Black plague coming to mind. The crucifixion affected billions. It was one of the key moments in history that had been at the forefront of Christian belief for over two millennia. The resurrection had been the one event that was divine and linked to Catholicism for the future.

Once Isaac arrived, he exited the taxi and walked up to small hill that the Romans had called the Skull. This hill is very close the Church of the Holy Sepulcher. It has been much disputed amongst scholars whether this was the exact location of the crucifixion. Isaac knew it to be the true site though.

He stayed for a while and watched tourists and locals visit the site. Some were on their knees praying, others were standing. One woman was on her hands and knees wailing. This was always an odd place for him to visit. He felt as though he belonged, but he also felt like an outsider. After an hour passed, he was ready to leave and go about his day. He left the hill at Golgotha in saddened state of mind.

42.

George and John were sitting outside of Isaac's house in their rental car. They had been there since yesterday on a stakeout. When George called Angelica after her shower the previous day, they had been parked only 200 feet away. They followed the two of them from the airport. The moment they had details of Isaac and Angelica's flight, George and John purchased their own tickets on the same flight. George wanted to stay within sight of Isaac when he arrived in Israel because they didn't have any lodging details. They would not have been able to find him again without knowing where he was staying. Luckily, they never saw one another on the plane,

By following them so closely, the two men came to realize that Isaac had a home here. George knew that he lived in Israel as a boy before his family moved to the States. He remembered the story from Vietnam. After watching the house for over a day, he had to admit that it was a nice place.

Through some of his more unlawful connections, John was able to purchase a sound amplifier when they arrived in Israel. It resembled a tiny umbrella, designed to hear through walls. It worked perfectly. Yesterday, as they sat in the car listening, they heard Isaac moving some furniture around. It was obviously heavy, as they heard him grunting while he was doing it. Then there was a creaking door sound. After a few minutes they heard the creaky door sound again and the furniture moving again. They wondered what he had been up to.

George and John slunk down in their rental car. John told his dad to grab a taxi and find a hotel room somewhere, but George was having none of that. He felt he could handle a stakeout just as well as John could. They hunkered down with some snacks and coffee, peeing in the bushes afterwards. They wanted to go into the house while the couple went to dinner, but there were too many people around the home that evening. The house was close to some local tourist destinations, so there was a lot of foot traffic. By the time the tourists stopped coming around, it was dark, and they didn't know when Isaac and Angelica would return.

In the morning, after Isaac left to go run some errands, they watched Angelica locking the front door to go shopping for clothes. They had heard all the conversations about Isaac going to the market and Angelica going to the dress shop. Unfortunately, they also heard their lovemaking the night before as well. But now the house was empty, and no tourists were around. It was their chance to go in.

The house was secluded, and the front door was not in sight of anyone. The two men went through the unlocked gate. As they approached the door, John pulled out his kit. Every good P.I. had a kit for picking locks. John went to work, and within 40 seconds they were in. George looked around for an alarm but didn't see one. They were in business.

The home was modest and open-concept, rustic décor with minimal belongings. You could tell instantly that this was not someone's everyday home. George thought the place seemed old, not that he was an expert on homes, especially in the Middle East. There was a bit of a musty smell, kind of like an old damp cellar.

They didn't know what to look for, except evidence of some sort to show who Isaac really was, anything substantial to confirm their suspicions. If there was any evidence, it would be hidden, they knew, so that Angelica, or anyone else wouldn't stumble on it. They looked around for a door remembering the creaking sound. But there were no doors, just open doorways, and cupboards.

"Johnny, remember we heard him move something big right before the creaking sound?"

"Yes. What are you thinking? The table? It's the only piece of furniture that would be heavy enough to make someone grunt while moving it."

They looked at each other. Then each of them grabbed a corner and started pushing the table off the carpet. Sure enough, there was that same sound that they heard yesterday, the table legs scraping the floor after it was pushed off the carpet, John rolled the carpet away, revealing a door cut into the floorboards. The door was steel but painted the same color as the wood. In the middle of it is a handle with a keypad. George frowned. He thought they'd come to a dead end.

"The keypad isn't set. The power light was off," John said, with a little surprise in his voice. Isaac did not strike him as someone who was careless enough not to lock a secret door. He grabbed the handle and pulled. Creaking sounds came from the hinges. Once the door was lifted all the way, a sensor light came on, revealing a stainless-steel ladder. They looked at each other.

"What is this? A storm cellar?" John queried.

Before he got an answer, his dad was already halfway down the ladder. More motion-sensor lights came on from below as the old man climbed further into the depths. John followed, first looking around to make sure the coast was clear. After all, they were at anyone's mercy now with a trap door above their heads. Once he felt they were in the clear, he joined his dad in the room below.

John looked toward his father as he stepped off the ladder. George's mouth was open in amazement. The two men looked around in awe of what they were seeing.

"What is this? A museum? A shrine? Look at all this stuff, Dad! There's millions of dollars in valuables here!"

"Yeah. I see that," George replied anxiously.

They were amazed at what they saw, there were gold coins, rubies, civil war guns, armor, even some priceless old baseball cards. One that stood out to George was an old Mickey Mantle rookie card from 1951. There were many books that seemed incredibly old as well, most of them were Bibles and individual Gospels. There was an old Don

Quixote collection as well. George saw what looked to be a Hebrew prayer shawl, a gold cross, and some dusty photo albums.

George started looking through one of the photo albums. After a few pages he stopped. What he had found astounded him. "Johnny, come here! Look!"

"What is it?"

"The proof we've been looking for."

The men turned page after page, looking at various black and white photos of Isaac posing with different people, and some by himself. There was one where he was in an old turn-of-the-century Ford, another where he was with two men, who they suspected were the Wright brothers standing beside the Wright Flyer.

"Could it be?" George said aloud.

"Sure, looks that way."

All the old photos showed Isaac with a scar. The pictures got progressively newer as the pages turned, and then he saw it. George was looking at a photo of himself standing beside Isaac, or Cris, as he was called then. It was a similar photo to the one that he had.

John looked at his dad and asked, "Saigon?"

"Yes, the same day my photo was taken if I remember correctly," George was elated. This photo was the most important piece of proof that they needed. George felt vindicated. All this travelling across the world for the last week was stressful. Thad hey almost died. Now they had verification that their quest was not a waste of time. George's confidence level just went through the roof.

John, continuing to search, opened a cabinet. Inside, he found a painting of Isaac in renaissance clothing. The date at the bottom was 1483 with a signature that couldn't be made out due to fading, most likely from age.

With all this stuff, George felt that they had the confirmation they needed to confront Isaac, or Cris, or whoever he wanted to call himself. George was quite sure that none of those names had been real.

John was looking at an old gospel, which was inside a clear glass box. The outside of the box had plenty of dust on it, but the inside was dust free. After studying it for a moment, he realized it was the Gospel of Matthew, and it seemed like an original, based on how old it looked. George looked at the gospel in his son's hand and the Hebrew cloth, he raised an eyebrow. He then looked at the Roman armor behind him. Thoughts started racing through his mind, unbelievable thoughts, and then he suddenly went very pale.

John saw something in his father's face. It was a look synonymous with fear, shock, and disbelief.

"Dad, what's wrong?" he asked nervously.

"Johnny, I know who he is!"

43.

Angelica arrived at the clothing store only to find it was closed. "Dammit," she growled. She really wanted that gown to wear tonight. "Oh well," she thought, maybe she'd come back later. The sign was in Hebrew, so she couldn't tell what time the shop opened. There were no other clothing stores around. She decided to head back to the house. The day was warm but not stifling yet. The walk back wouldn't be too hot. She figured by mid-afternoon it would be sweltering.

After the 10-minute walk, she arrived back at the house. Upon entering, she saw the dining table had been moved, and what looked like a part of the floor was lifted. She figured there was a cellar, and Isaac came back early doing something down there. She heard voices as she approached the open floor hatch. not Isaac's voice though. Suddenly, she felt a little nervous wondering if these were intruders. She started to back away. Then she recognized one of the voices.

"George!" she said to herself.

She quietly stepped closer to the opened door and listened as George and John talked about jewels, gold, and other valuables. After a few minutes of eavesdropping, she heard George say, "I know who he is!"

Slowly, she climbed down the ladder, and as she stepped into the room, she asked, "So, who is he?"

George turned in alarm. "Angelica! You startled us," John said.

"What are you doing here?" Her eyes flashed surprise. "You can't be here. This is breaking and entering." She paused as she started looking around at all the priceless treasures and asked, "Oh my God, what is all of this?"

"This is proof! Proof of what we've been saying all along, Isaac is incredibly old," George announced arrogantly.

She was feeling anxious, as she felt deceitful again, as well as knowing that Isaac would be home in a while. But her curiosity won over. "What proof?"

"Here, look," George said shakily. He was still unnerved from what he had been about to reveal to John before they were interrupted. He handed the photo album to Angelica, with the black and white photos of Isaac over the last century.

"So, now that you've seen these, do you still think it's a coincidence, it can't be! I mean why would he have all these old photos of some lookalike? It's him! And here, look!" He turned the page to the photo of himself with Isaac in Vietnam. "This shows that he knew me." He pointed, with just a little bit of self-satisfaction.

"This is insanity," she said vibrantly. "How old is he?"

"Very old, much older than I expected if what I am thinking is correct."

They both looked at George puzzled.

"Just hear me out. Where are we? We're in the Holy Land, right?"

They both nodded their heads and said, "Yes." in unison.

"Right, the Holy Land, which was under Roman Occupation 2000 years ago. Look over there. You see that Hebrew scarf? And that cross? Also look at the manuscript we found, its Matthew's Gospel! I'm no expert," he said, making a side glance to Angelica, "but I'm guessing it's the original."

This caught Angelica's attention. She was a curator after all. "Let me see that please."

He handed it to her eagerly.

"I've never seen a manuscript like this. It's so old. If this is the earliest version, it would be absolutely priceless."

Just then she caught a glimpse of the Renaissance painting on the wall. "Oh my God, that's a Botticelli, and it's a portrait of Isaac! That's from the 1400's! It's precious."

George chimed in, "Everything in this room is precious. Isaac is precious. Don't you see?"

"See what?" she asked.

Taking a deep breath to explain, he began.

"Who or what person in history, in all the books you've read, all the stories you've heard, what person, if any, would have the miraculous ability to be immortal?"

They just looked at him.

He continued, "Religion is everywhere in this room, Gospels, the scarf, evidence of stuff going back a long time. Tell me, who would that be?"

There was some hesitancy on Angelica's face, and John's. They knew where George was going with this and clearly sensed his final point on the matter. But the thought was unimaginable. Everyone's face was pale, yet nobody wanted to answer the question.

"Fine, I'll say it."

"Say what?!" said the man that was now standing on the ladder.

They all turned, shocked to see Isaac watching them from the ladder. They had all been so consumed by what George was trying to say, that Isaac was able to enter the vault unnoticed, just like Angelica had minutes earlier.

44.

None of them spoke.

Angelica looked nervously at Isaac, startled and ashamed to be caught trespassing. George's last words had just spooked her a little as well.

Isaac was unsure how long they had been in the room and what they had seen. He had been alerted by his alarm company that the motion sensors in his vault had been triggered, and he rushed back as quickly as he could. Even so, it had been long enough to be troublesome.

"What are you doing here, George? This has gone far enough. These are my personal things, and your constant intrusion is starting to piss me off. You've broken into my home, invaded my privacy? What gives you the right?" he asked angrily.

George replied, just as angrily, "You gave me the right, Cris, when you took off in 1972! Now, I run into my old friend in Florida who's alive and well, looking the same as he was 47 years ago, when, in fact, you should be dead?! That's what gave me the right! I know who you are. We all know who you are," he said factually.

Angelica looked back and forth between the two men as they verbally sparred, not knowing what to think or do. She glanced over to John, who was taking in the scene silently. Still unsure, but feeling she needed to intervene, Angelica spoke.

"Isaac, there is what seems to be irrefutable proof here that you don't age. There is a photo of you and George together in this photo album from 1972. There are other photos that look over 100 years old. And the painting of you has a 1483 date on it. Isaac, please, tell us what's going on?"

Then George said, "I don't know whether I should bow down before you or not."

"What are you talking about?" Isaac asked.

"You are the King of Kings! The Messiah! The lord Jesus Christ! It's not that you have arisen, like the Bible said you would. There wasn't a second coming. You just never left! I understand the cloak and dagger now. I understand the lies, and why you went away after you were shot. This is all part of something bigger."

All of them were watching for Isaac's reaction.

Calmly, Isaac asked, "Why do you think I'm him?"

"Well, come on! Clearly, you've been alive for a long, long time, and you can't be killed. We watched you get blown up, only to be perfectly fine a minute later! You're a hero in Spain and Madrid. We also found out about 9/11 and Hurricane Katrina. I bet in over 2000 years; you've saved thousands of lives. Now, we find this room with all these things going back to the time of Christ, the time of you! These are just the things we know for sure. You go where you're needed, and you do what you must, right? Who else would have immortality and know what's going to happen in future events, if not Jesus?"

"What do you want from me George?" Isaac asked suspiciously.

"The truth! Look," George said, as he took a deep breath to calm himself down, "I didn't plan on all this happening, but that day in the bank changed everything."

"Yes, it did," Isaac thought ruefully. He looked at George and knew that this man would never let it go, none of them would now. Why hadn't he locked the vault?! He had to say something.

"George, I hated leaving you. You were one of the best friends I ever had," he admitted.

This was the first confirmation they had from Isaac since this all began.

"I went to the field hospital on the chopper, but the wound healed even before you strapped me on the stretcher. You just didn't notice because the blood was still on my uniform. Once I arrived at the hospital, I left as soon as the doctors were out of sight. I had no choice.

Obviously, this kind of thing couldn't easily be explained. I've always thought of you George. I was happy to see that you were still alive that day at the bank. Angelica, please, stop looking at me like that!"

Angelica, who had been listening intently, said, "I'm sorry. I just can't believe what I'm hearing."

"Well, I'll explain it to you, but it's not going to be what you all think. I was born here in Judea. Supposedly, I died at the age of 33. I've not grown older since then, and yes, that was over 2000 years ago. And I've walked the Earth ever since. No, I didn't really die. Well, maybe I did. But I awoke after I should have been dead. I left after that and moved around a lot. And as time went on, I would change my name frequently. I moved when I had to, so people wouldn't notice that my face didn't age."

"What about all the bad things that happen when you go somewhere?" John interrupted.

"I'm getting to that. After I supposedly died, I started getting this compulsory pull to certain events, Acts-of-God events, man-made disasters, wars, and conflicts. I wouldn't know what was about to happen. I would just suddenly know where I had to go. For example, when I had to be in Barcelona last week, I didn't know why, but once the plane crashed, I did. The same thing happened with Madrid and 9/11." As he spoke, the three of them were all mesmerized by what he was saying.

"You see, the bad things aren't about me, and they don't happen to me specifically. I'm drawn there. I am supposed to see it, to see the destruction, death, and suffering. It's my punishment. These bad things would happen whether I was there or not. George, I wasn't drafted to go to Vietnam. I was drawn there, so I enlisted."

Angelica asked, "A punishment?"

"Yes."

"Punishment for what?"

At that moment, they heard noises coming from upstairs. The Israeli police had shown up. Isaac had forgotten that he had called them when he was alerted by the alarm company. "Down here!" he said to the officers who were now looking through the floor entrance with their guns drawn.

"You called the police?" John asked nervously.

"Of course, I did. This stuff is valuable as you can see. I didn't know if I was getting robbed or not. You did break in after all, although I should have known it was the two of you."

"We didn't see an alarm?" John asked curiously.

"The vault has motion sensors," he replied.

The police yelled for everyone to come out. After they climbed back up the ladder, Isaac showed the proof he was the homeowner and the one who called them. Despite George and John's protests, the police put them into handcuffs and took them outside to their cars. Isaac was told to come to give a statement and press charges. He said he would be by the police headquarters in an hour.

Angelica looked at him incredulously. "You can't press charges Isaac. They just wanted answers. They weren't going to steal anything."

He waited until George and John were out of ear shot. Isaac took her softly by the shoulders but with a sharpness in his voice, "I know, I'm not going to press charges, but an hour or two in an Israeli jail cell may teach them not to be so nosy next time."

45.

After about an hour (which Isaac felt was a suitable amount of time for George and John to stew in a cell.) He called for a taxi to drive them to the police station. Angelica had been quiet during that hour. Isaac assumed she was still processing what she had just learned in the vault. She and the Watsons had had a shock, he knew. They now knew the world was not what it seemed and that things existed beyond their imagination, supernatural things. It wasn't every day you learn that a man you thought you knew, was immortal. He could sense her unrest.

At the police station, they went to the desk, and he asked for the sergeant. When the officer came, Isaac explained that he didn't want to press charges. The sergeant said that they would have to free the two men if there were no charges laid. Isaac shook his head in understanding.

"Can you give them this note after you release them, please?" he asked.

The Sergeant nodded and took the note.

"Come on, we need to go somewhere," Isaac said to Angelica.

"Where?"

"Golgotha!"

George and John were confused when they were released, and even more so when an Israeli officer handed them a note. John read it out loud, "*Call a taxi. Ask the driver to take you to Church of the Holy Sepulcher in Golgotha ... Cris.*"

"Golgotha?" John said to his dad. George shrugged.

The sergeant, overhearing their question, said gruffly, "That's where Jesus was crucified." The two men looked at each other puzzled.

"I guess we're going to Golgotha," George said emphatically.

Once Angelica and Isaac were dropped off, they walked up to the Church of the Holy Sepulcher. She looked at him quizzically and asked, "Now what?"

"Now, we wait for the Watsons," he replied.

46.

The Watson father and son team exited the taxi at Golgotha and headed on foot up the hill. They were extremely interested to know why Isaac asked them there, as well as why he didn't press charges, although George was relieved. He had been worried for John, thinking he could have had a criminal record because his old man dragged him on this manhunt.

The two men located Isaac and Angelica in the distance, standing away from the crowds, which were abundant. They walked over to meet them.

"Hello, George," Isaac said sternly. "Thanks for coming."

"Thanks for not pressing charges," George replied.

"You're welcome. I know you were just looking for answers. I can't blame you for that; however, you're both very annoying and persistent. I wanted to teach you a lesson. Having said that, I suppose I do owe you a full disclosure. I'm going to tell you all a story. It's an old story, some of which you've heard about probably in Sunday school. Most of this story took place very close to here, and it ended right over there with a crucifixion."

"Way back in 33 A.D., the Jewish authorities known as the Sanhedrin were threatened by a Rabbi. This Rabbi had been preaching to the people, and he had his disciples as you well know. The Roman Governor, Pontius Pilate oversaw the district. Pilate was a feared leader, and he had complete rule of the region, answering only to the Emperor Tiberius. Pontius Pilate was going to great lengths to put an end to the preaching's, at the request of the Sanhedrin high priests. The priests struck a deal with one of the disciples to betray his friend to capture him. For a small payment, the betrayer was to reveal who this Rabbi was by kissing him on the cheek. Then the Temple guards took the Rabbi into custody in the Garden of Gethsemane. That's the story of Jesus' capture to the Romans, orchestrated by The Sanhedrin Priests and Pontius Pilate."

George said, "Yes, we are all familiar with the story. Everyone knows that the apostle Judas betrayed Jesus with a kiss. However, it was interesting hearing it first-hand." George cocked his eyebrow knowingly.

"Yeah, about that, George. That's where you have it wrong. This is a first-hand point of view, for sure. However, I'm not who you think I am."

"What are you talking about? You just told the story as if you were there."

"I was there! But, George, ask yourself, why am I being punished? Why would God punish his son for such a long period of time so harshly? I'm not Jesus, George. My birth name was Judas Iscariot."

47.

George's eyes widened, and he took a moment to process what he had just heard, they all did. The silence was deafening. They had all been thinking one thing, and then the truth went in the complete opposite direction. Then George spoke, "You're Judas Iscariot, as in Judas, the Betrayer?"

"The same, yes."

They were all silent. Isaac was not at all surprised that their processing of this information would take a bit longer.

He continued, "I guess God decided I needed to be punished infinitely for my disloyalty. In the Gospels, it states that I betrayed Jesus in the Garden of Gethsemane. That's when the Temple Guards seized him. He was then turned over to Governor Pontius Pilate, who then ordered his crucifixion, reluctantly, but he was under pressure from the Sanhedrin. I betrayed my friend and rabbi for a mere 30 silver coins. The centuries have not numbed my pain. I still feel great sorrow for what I had done." Isaac had an anguished look on his face as if remembering the exact moment of his betrayal.

"So, you see, I'm not a hero. I'm a villain. I truly didn't know they would crucify him! But I deserve the punishment handed down to me. Jesus was made a martyr. And I was judged a betrayer and to some, a murderer. I tried to give back the silver coins to the priests, but I was disregarded." Angelica, George, and John continued to listen intently.

Isaac resumed, "Some history books state that I hung myself, and other chronicles say I jumped off a cliff. Both stories have a little truth to them. I did try to hang myself, from a tree branch that hung near a Cliffside. But as I felt myself slipping away, the branch broke, and I fell over the cliff. The fall was more than 200 feet. When I awoke below on rocks beside a river, I looked up at the tree, the rope still around my neck attached to the broken branch beside me. Two hundred feet I fell. I should have died, but the only mark on me was the scar on my neck from the rope. And in my hand was this silver coin."

The three of them were listening to his story keenly. Angelica said, "Do you mean to tell us that you've been watching people die for over 2000 years, going through repeated torment and calamity as your punishment?"

"Yes, exactly."

"How did you deal with this for 2000 years? This would drive someone to insanity."

"Angelica, in those early years, I tried to take my life more times than I can count, of course, without success. I didn't deal with it very well; I suppose you could say."

"That's awful. But you've been helping people."

"Yes, I made a mistake. Probably, the biggest mistake in history. I am the original villain, but I'm still human. I may have done what I did partially out of greed, but mostly out of fear and anger. Jesus and I were at odds. I believed in what he was doing, but I was afraid of the danger he put us into with his preaching. I didn't want him to die though. That was never my intention. I was his closest friend, until that day. I was one of his 12 disciples! I cared about people. I always have. And I never want to see anyone hurt. So yes, I do help them. God has handed down this punishment. My penance is to help those that I can. I believe, because I was the cause of the greatest hurt to the best of his people; therefore, I get summoned to all those disasters and that's why I can't ever die."

Angelica had tears in her eyes. She saw him looking at her, and she walked up and hugged him. This was not the response he had expected at all. "I am so sorry for you, sorry for the torment that has burdened you for eternity."

"Thank you," he said softly, "I deserved what I got. However, I feel that Pontius Pilate deserved some of the blame as well. I feel that he got away with taking two lives, mine, and Jesus. This is the first time in my long life that I've admitted to someone of my deed. George, you're a persistent man. Angelica, that's why sometimes I'm a little distant." He pushed her away from him a bit so he could look at her. "You see, I have had two different families in my life. They all died. It's a problem falling in love or having friends because everyone eventually dies. But the worst is watching your child die. It hurts so much to lose those close to me, so I tend not to let anyone in. After my betrayal, I left. That wasn't easy because I had a wife at that time and two boys. I had to leave them behind. I would have brought them nothing but shame if I stayed. After I fell and survived, I realized that I had to leave. But I had to give my family closure. Hence, I spread the word to people, who didn't personally know me, that Judas killed himself. They believed his body was washed away by the river."

"That sounds very sad and lonely," she said. "I'm sorry about your families. That must have been unbearable."

"It was so long ago, but yes, it still hurts. I didn't get to say goodbye."

"The coin I saw you looking at in the car, is it one of the thirty silver pieces? It's from the same era," Angelica asked.

"Yes, and only a few days prior, I had left it at your auction house. But then I felt it in my pocket while waiting for you in the car, thousands of miles away across the ocean. It's a constant reminder of my terrible deed."

"Coin? What coin?" George asked. "The same coin you gave me as we tied you down on the chopper?"

"Yes, the same. But it came back to me the next day, like it always does. It hasn't left me in 2000 years," Isaac sighed.

John asked, "Isaac, I did a search on you, and all evidence of your existence as Isaac Rojas disappeared before 2005. So, every few years you just re-invent yourself and start over somewhere else?"

"Precisely," Isaac said. "More than a few years though. I would try to stay somewhere at least 15 years. I thought that was a good time frame for people not to notice too much change in my face. I would pay a lot of money for fake passports and IDs. The more you pay, the better they work. I would even pay more than asking to ensure the forger's silence. I will let you in on another little secret: in all these years, I have always used just the letters from my original name of 'Judas Iscariot' into my fake names. Some of the names I took sounded kind of funny - for example Cris, I mean, who spells Cris without an H in it?" he laughed a little. "I've reused the same names frequently, like Isaac and Darius. They're the ones I'm most fond of. I can't use my original name for obvious reasons but using the same letters keeps me in touch with where I came from."

George said, "What you did so long ago was regrettable, but you've made up for it, the lives you've saved, all those people you helped. You're a good man, I can see that. Maybe, God chose you. Maybe, you were supposed to betray Jesus, and, maybe, he was always meant to be a martyr. Christianity says he was. I'm a Christian, and I go to church, not as often as I should. I'll go more now though, let me tell you that much."

"Why is that?" Isaac asked suspiciously.

"Well, until ten minutes ago, I was never 100 percent sure that God existed. I mean, yes, I believed, but is anyone ever sure of something they can't see or touch? Now, I'm looking at a living breathing miracle. If that isn't divine, then I don't know what is."

"Divine, I don't know. But, yes, there are greater things out there beyond the scope of normal reasoning. I don't know if being alive for so long is a miracle. However, yes, George, it shows you something more is at work."

"What about the collection in your vault?" John asked Isaac.

"Ahhh, yes, well, some of them are keep sakes, and others are just items that I'll eventually sell, mostly memories, I guess. A lot of them are a means to an end. You see, I can't work a 9-5 job, when you constantly get summoned to leave suddenly. I still must live though, so I sell stuff occasionally. Travelling the world to disasters isn't cheap, and neither is moving around a lot. A good fake passport costs about $10.000."

"What about the Roman Broadsword you sold?" Angelica asked.

"It was given to me in 406 by a Roman General for saving his child. Most of these things, I would sell. They're just things. It's all part of something bigger, like you said, George."

George, John, and Angelica were all still in a bit of shock at everything they had just heard, but they were taking it well considering the uniqueness of the situation. Isaac knew it was a lot to process. He hoped that they could move past this. Revealing this for the first time made him feel good. He hadn't expected that. He wondered now if he and George could continue their friendship 47 years later. He hoped so. He also wondered about his relationship with Angelica, now with her knowing who he really was and that she would grow older, while he would not. That was a lot to contemplate. Angelica had an extremely curious look on her face. "What was he like?" she asked innocently.

Isaac laughed a little. "I was waiting for one of you to ask me that. I'm surprised it took this long," he said curiously.

"Yeshua or Rabbi was what we called him. He was a true leader. People followed him not just because they needed someone to follow, but because he was such a powerful presence. He would answer questions in ways that nobody ever expected. He wouldn't give you the answer you wanted; it would be the answer you needed. His insight was nothing short of spectacular. He was kind and empathetic. To Yeshua, no one person was bigger or more important than another. Everyone was equal. I loved him deeply as a friend, and I followed him. Unfortunately, the political hierarchies were threatened by his preaching. I tried to get him to tone it down, and this is where we disagreed. I felt horrible about that. I had not realized how much of an impression he had made on his followers." Isaac glanced up with a smile, "George, you come in at a close second place."

They all laughed at his comment.

George asked, "So, what now?"

"Nothing. You all go on about your lives, and I go on about mine. It's that simple. I hope that we can all stay in touch."

"I would really like to continue our friendship, Isaac. Or Cris," George laughed a bit.

"Call me Isaac. Cris is no more. Just don't call me Judas. That name doesn't go over too well." Again, they all laughed. "I'd like to be friends again, George, very much."

"I guess, if we continue to spend time together, I'll need a good plastic surgeon," Angelica stated with a twinkle in her eye.

Isaac rolled his eyes, "Oh, you're just a regular comedian now, aren't you?"

She just smiled wickedly.

He told them to take some time to process everything, and in the meantime, he'd go back to the house to clean and wait for them there.

The thought of Judas Iscariot cleaning struck George as kind of funny, a 2000-year-old immortal apostle, doing something as mundane as cleaning. George decided then and there that he liked Isaac. He didn't really care about his dark past and hoped to rekindle their old friendship. George knew Isaac, was a good man, conflicted, but righteous and steadfast, not a bad guy to have on your side.

48.

After Isaac left to go back to his home, the three of them found a place to sit and discuss everything Isaac had just told them. The world as they knew it had just been turned completely upside down. After all, it's not every day you get concrete proof that there really is a God, and that miraculous things really do exist. Information like this can, and usually does, change a person. The saying, God works in mysterious ways, really had an impact on them now.

They spent considerable time rehashing and trying to process the things they had just learned, Angelica sighed and said, "It really makes you wonder. I mean, will I be punished when the time comes for my judgement, for not being a devout Christian? Can I make up for lost time now before it's too late? I mean I am a believer in Christian theology, if there is a kingdom, will I be accepted?"

George shrugged and said, "Just live the best life you can Angelica."

One thing they all agreed upon was that Isaac deserved forgiveness. They didn't know if God would ever forgive him, but THEY could. Maybe it was never punishment. Judas may have always been the chosen one to set in motion the events that solidified the beginning of Christianity.

Isaac was back at his home waiting for the others. He was recapping the day's events, and everything else as his thoughts drifted to rationalize his life.

He once again felt pity for himself while thinking of his special circumstance. People could never understand what it was really like to be immortal. There would come a time when a limit would be reached from living a perpetual life, and you would want to check out of this mortal coil.

Imagine living 30 times longer than the average human. You would have experienced everything that could have ever been done, in some cases many times over. Food would lose its flavor. Love would lose its luster, and you would inevitably bury all the people you ever cared about. There would be nothing left to quicken you, to motivate you. Suppose you had a best friend, only they were the twentieth best friend in your life, and that person would eventually die as well, all the while not ever knowing the real you. Envision planting roots only to have to leave them all behind every 15 years, so that no one figured out that you were different. Such anguish. Isaac couldn't help but think that people who desired to live forever had not really thought it out completely. He, and all his aliases, had experienced this world to the fullest degree.

He remembered the first 500 years, they were the hardest, when trying to become accustomed to his situation was nearly impossible. During those early years, he tried repeatedly to kill himself, only to be denied every time. Life became sour. His only real pleasure from his longevity was saving people.

Around the 1500's, the new world had been discovered, and within a hundred years, he was travelling by sea to the Americas and other continents. He journeyed everywhere and learned the cultures of all the indigenous people. He travelled with the Spanish Armada to South America. He spent years there as a foreigner, learning their ways. He also lived in Australia in the late 1800's when it was a penal colony, on the cusp of becoming its own nation. He was in America during both the revolutionary war of the 1700's, and later the civil war

Eventually, travelling became the one thing that he did, and did well. Whenever he was summoned to a location, he always tried to discover that new place and their culture, after he dealt with whatever disastrous event was occurring first. It was during that time that he learned so much more about the world, the things that eluded him for the first 1500 years. It rejuvenated his spirit, for a while anyway, but now he had seen it all again, too many times. The world was too small for an immortal. How much longer would he have to endure?

Upon coming out of his self-pitied inner thoughts there was a jolt, and abruptly he felt it, the pull. His emotions were suddenly that of shock because the vision he received in his mind was from Golgotha and the roadway surrounding. He immediately got up and went for the front door. As he ran, his phone rang, it was George calling.

After a long deep conversation between the three of them in Golgotha, they were going to hail some taxis. George and John desperately needed to shower after spending the night in a car staking out Isaac's home and sitting in a cell for two hours. Angelica was to head back to see Isaac. Her taxi came first, and she departed. As John and George discussed a bit more about the recent revelations and waited for their taxi, they unexpectedly heard a loud screech of tires followed by a crashing sound of metal and debris. To their shock, they realized it was Angelica's taxi that had just been T-boned by a van while merging into traffic. They hurried over to the crash site only to find her taxi was completely flipped over. The horrific scene had George frantically wondering if Angelica had survived. Many bystanders were assisting, trying to get the car doors open. They pulled the taxi driver out to safety, but Angelica was still trapped. John and some others were doing their best to get to her, but to no avail. She was stuck inside and unresponsive. George quickly took out his cell phone and called Isaac.

49.

George called Isaac to tell him about the accident. Isaac already knew something was wrong, but to find out Angelica was hurt and trapped was not what he anticipated. He had never received a summons about someone that he knew before. George instructed him to take the rental car that he and John left behind after getting arrested at the house. He said the keys were under the visor.

Only minutes passed before Isaac came in brakes screeching to the crash site. The overturned car was now surrounded by firemen and police. They were using the jaws of life to get the door open to the back seat. The gruesome scene horrified him. He usually never felt scared or helpless. This was different because it was someone that he cared for deeply. He could see Angelica through the broken window, motionless, bleeding from the forehead and pale. In that moment, he thought, "What have I done?!" He could not help but think she wouldn't have been here if he had not invited her to come. He felt responsible. Why, after thousands of disasters, couldn't he just once be sent somewhere with the knowledge to prevent one of them? George could clearly see the anguish in Isaac's face, the helplessness.

The firemen got the door of the taxi off and pulled Angelica from the crushed vehicle. She was then put onto a stretcher and moved to the ambulance. The paramedics would not allow anyone to ride along. Isaac's facial expression had now changed from helplessness to anger. George asked him to come with them to the hospital.

"There is nothing I can do for her there. I'm too late," he yelled. "There is something I will do though," Isaac said precisely.

50

Isaac turned away from the crash site. He started walking back toward the Church of the Holy Sepulcher. George followed with John in tow. Once he got close to the church, he walked past it to a hilled area, he knew of it as the exact location of where the crucifixion took place. Once there, he stopped and bent over. George and John stayed back and observed him.

Isaac dropped to his knees and let out wretched garbled moan as he threw a bunch of dirt that he picked up toward the sky. "Have I not been in your servitude long enough?" he yelled angrily at the top of his lungs. "What else can I do? I've done all that you required of me, and more. Why have you forsaken me? I didn't know they would kill him! I DIDN'T KNOW! Please, spare her! I'm begging you! Take me instead! Isn't that what you want? It's me who did it!" He paused for a few moments, then he said, "I'M SORRY!", repeating it over and over. The suffering in his trembling voice was unbearable to hear as George watched this man fall apart. George could see that the millennia had taken their toll on his soul. He was at the breaking point. George couldn't help but feel for the man. He heard the heart-wrenching agony and long suppressed despair, filled with centuries of pain coming to light. The life he had led, the things he had seen, all coming to a head now at this time. George sensed that this was the first time he has addressed his punisher in such a way, the accusatory tone in his voice and the hatred was evident. It wasn't hatred for God, it was hatred for himself, for what he had done. George knew there was no coincidence here. Why would Angelica get hurt here, and now, in Golgotha of all places, right after Isaac revealed himself to them?

George walked up behind Isaac and assisted him to his feet. "Come on, old friend," he said, "We need to go to the hospital."

51

The three of them left Golgotha in the rental car and went to the hospital where Angelica was taken. Isaac was nervous along the way. He sat in the back seat while John drove, and George rode shotgun. They were giving him as much space as he needed. The man was usually in control when things went awry. However, he always dealt with situations that were not personal like this time. George thought sadly, "If Isaac met his breaking point, how much punishment could someone receive before they lose their wits? His exceptional life was the most incredible thing he had ever heard of, and he felt honored to be his friend, no matter who he was originally. We all make mistakes. His was just made against the wrong person. But he paid his dues."

Angelica was still unconscious with a concussion and some minor contusions to the head and face. The doctor said that there was minimal swelling and that she would recover nicely in the next few days to a week. X-Rays and a CT scan all looked promising. Isaac was relieved, as were the Watsons.

Isaac stayed at the hospital overnight and slept in the chair next to Angelica's bed. He woke up to her speaking to him in the morning. The words he heard were, "My hero." He knew that meant there was no brain damage or amnesia from the head trauma. They exchanged hugs, and she apologized for not wearing her seat belt in the taxi. Isaac laughed. He was just happy he hadn't lost her. Maybe, someone upstairs was listening to him after all. He decided to visit the hospital chapel afterwards. Some gratitude was in order, he felt.

52

November had arrived. Months passed since his reveal in Jerusalem and the accident. He was back in Florida, and Angelica was in New York. They talked regularly and saw each other as often as they could. She was even considering coming to live the beach life with him on the Floridian coast. She was flying in for a few days next weekend, and he hoped they would discuss it further. Isaac was still a little apprehensive about the pain that would come with outliving her. But they were already close friends and lovers, so that was going to happen regardless. They would just deal with it when that time came.

George visited a few times as well. They usually met next door at the Frittery. After all, he lived only a half hour away from Isaac, hence the reason they ran into each other at the bank that fateful day. John occasionally accompanied his dad, and Isaac even got to meet George's granddaughter, Penelope. Both Isaac and George were glad to be in touch again after 47 years apart. They usually talked about Vietnam or sports, not too much about Isaac's identity. But George did sometimes ask if he had been summoned to any disasters lately, especially, if something had been in the news recently. Isaac told him that nothing had come up since Angelica's accident. There had been times where he went months without a summons, and that was the nature of the beast, so to speak. This most recent hiatus was particularly long though.

Isaac often told George and Angelica about some of his adventures over his lifetime. He did after all have two millennia of stories built up. It felt good to be able to share some of it after having kept them to himself for so long. They were always interested in his past. Imagine getting information about historical events by someone that was there, in real time. Isaac told George that he saw a documentary about Judas from National Geographic. It stated that there was a gospel of Judas found in the 1970's. There was no truth to it. He had never written a gospel. The documentary even talked about the relationship between him and Jesus. Isaac expressed to them that they had been friends up until the day of his betrayal. He found it humorous that 2000 years of hearsay could be so easily misconstrued.

During the most recent time that the two men had met, George looked at him in silence for a minute, thinking hard about what he would say. He wanted to ask some hard questions. "Are you satisfied with the life you've led? Are you happy?" he asked.

Isaac replied, "Well I'm not sad. I have happy moments, and I enjoy life. Are you wondering if I want to die? The answer is yes, but not right now. I just wish to live out a normal life. I don't like starting over every 10 to 15 years, and I don't like not having longtime friends, or someone to love. Seeing all the death that I've seen, makes me sad, but, unfortunately, you get used to it. I feel satisfied about the people that I was able to help, especially the children. So, I guess, yes to both questions."

George stated, "I've spoken with the others, and we felt that you deserve forgiveness. We don't know if we're qualified to make that decision, but we forgave you for what you did. I don't know if that means anything, but you said that was the first time you admitted who you were and what you did. We hope that you can take some solace in that. We've heard your story, and none of us thinks of you as a villain. Like I said earlier, what happened to you seems as though it was preordained. In the Bible, it stated that Jesus said, one of his disciples would betray him. How would he have known that?"

Isaac replied directly, "He did say that, and he knew it was going to be me. In fact, he looked right at me when he said it. I'll never forget that."

53.

Angelica flew into Tampa International Airport, where Isaac picked her up, and brought her back to his antique shop.

Once she got settled, she grabbed a package out of her suitcase.

"I have a gift for you."

"Oh, wow! It's not my birthday. It's not even any of the several birth dates I've chosen for myself over the years!"

"Look who's the comedian now," she said with a smile. She noticed his personality had changed since Jerusalem. He was more relaxed, not as serious. This change was very enticing to her. The less secretive he was, the more attractive and vulnerable he became. She handed him the package. Isaac un-wrapped the paper and revealed a Roman broadsword.

"Oh my, this is stunning!" he said admirably as he ran his hands down the sheath while looking closely at its intricate detail.

"I couldn't afford the $327,000 to get yours back, and the new owner probably wouldn't have sold it anyway, so I didn't try. I know this one is not as old or as special to you, but it came into the auction house a few weeks ago. When I saw it, I immediately thought of you."

"Thank you! This means so much more to me than the other one because it came from you." He took her in his arms and kissed her passionately.

That afternoon, after some intimate time in his bed, they were having a late lunch on his patio overlooking the water. They were engaged in some great conversation about the past, as usual. Then suddenly, out of nowhere, it happened, again. He felt it, the summons.

She saw his brow furrow.

"What is it? What's wrong?" she asked apprehensively.

"I don't know. I have to go though."

"Go where?"

"That's just it. I don't think anywhere. I mean, I feel the pull like all the other times. But it feels different this time."

"Different, how?"

"I'm not sure. It's hard to explain. It's pulling me just over there, to the pier. And I don't feel the sense of doom and gloom that normally comes with it."

"So, I don't need to be concerned about a tsunami or a cruise ship crashing into the pier?"

"No. I mean, I don't know. I can't explain this, but I need to go there right now."

"I'm coming with you," she said.

He agreed. "Yes, I think you're supposed to come with me."

"Huh? What do you mean? It's telling you I should come?" she asked nervously.

He shrugged and took her hand. "Come on, let's go." They walked quickly down the patio stairs onto the sand and headed for the pier.

Angelica was not sure what to make of all this. She was a little hesitant, although equally curious and excited. She kept up with his quick pace.

They arrived at the pier and walked all the way to the end. He stood for a minute trying to figure out what was happening. Then he saw it.

His silver coin was sitting on the wooden railing. He walked up to it. It was his coin alright, looking the same as always. He'd last seen it that morning on his nightstand, as usual. Now oddly, it was here.

"Is that your coin?" Angelica asked, coming up behind him.

"Yes, and it's why I'm here; I think."

"What are you supposed to do?"

"Pick it up, I guess."

Once the coin was in his hand, he felt it, like a smack on the head. In fact, it jolted him so much that Angelica saw it as well.

"What was that?" she asked.

"I know what I have to do," he said plainly.

"What?"

"I'm supposed to throw it. I don't know why, but I need to throw it right now."

"So, throw it already! What are you waiting for?" she asked anxiously.

He looked at the coin, sensing this was the last time he would ever see it, and then with all his strength, he threw it hard, as though he was sending it across the whole Gulf of Mexico. They watched it sail through the air for what seemed like an eternity and then finally drop into the water.

And instantly he knew the finality of the moment. He knew it was over. He felt it as he had felt the pull a thousand times before. Only this time, it made him feel free. Released. Forgiven. Isaac told Angelica what he felt as they both stood there looking to where it dropped in the water. "It's over," he said with a long overdue sigh of relief. "I'm released." He turned to look at Angelica, and she saw something miraculous. Her eyes widened.

"Isaac, your scar!"

"What about it?"

"It's gone!"

He reached up and felt his neck where the scar had been since that day when he tried so long ago to hang himself. He couldn't feel it anymore, physically, or emotionally.

They stood there looking at each other for a long while. She could see his mind was racing a mile a minute trying to figure out what just happened. They both turned back to look at the water where the coin had landed.

"Why do you think it ended?" she asked.

"I'm not sure. Maybe, because I finally admitted to you all who I really was. Or, maybe, God just felt that I've served my time."

The November sunset was going down over the water. They put their arms around each other and watched it in silence. He knew that he would age now like a normal person and die like a normal person. But first, he would live, and love, like a normal person. This was a good day.

He looked down at Angelica, then up at the sky, and simply said, "Thank you."

THE END.

Epilogue

The old man sat in his wheelchair beside the pew. It was a rainy Tuesday morning in Tampa, the area known for its 300 plus days per year of sunshine. But today wasn't one of them.

Angelica was sitting beside him. She was smiling encouragingly at him, as was their daughter Kate. The three of them were there for confession. Isaac had never been inside a confessional before. Well, not as the confessor anyway. He was approximately 2069 years old, but everyone else knew him to be 87. But in all that time he hadn't felt the need to confess. God already knew of his greatest sin.

According to his neurologist, he had about three months to live. 46 years have passed since he was released from his sentence that day at the Florida pier. 46 years of love, family, and blissful aging. Seeing his face age in the mirror, watching wrinkles appear and his hair go from brown to gray to white, experiencing the aches and pains of his joints and muscles as they stiffened and declined, all of this he met with a smile. Now dying of an inoperable brain tumor, he felt it was time to confess before God, to formally start a conversation with him in person, in a way.

Angelica had gone first and then Kate. Now it was his turn. The church's maintenance manager unfolded the ramp for Isaac's wheelchair so Kate could move him smoothly into the booth. After a moment, there was some shuffling. Then the panel to the other side opened, and the priest spoke.

"Are you here to confess your sins before the Lord?" he asked.

"Yes, Father. Forgive me, for I have sinned," he sighed. "It's been a very long time since my last confession. Well, truthfully, Father, I've never been to confession."

"Well, my son, it's never too late to start. Please, begin."

"Yes, Father. Well, I've lied, I've betrayed, and I have taken lives in war and in self-defense. But most importantly, and to my ever-lasting shame, my actions caused the death of someone that was close to me a long, long time ago," he said solemnly.

"Responsibility has so many varying factors," the priest replied.

"Yes, but you see, Father, my long life is coming to an end. I know you're going to think I'm out of my mind for saying this, but I need to get something off my chest, something unbelievable, yet absolutely true." He paused for a few seconds. "My real name is Judas Iscariot. I was born in Judea over 2000 years ago. And I betrayed my friend. My betrayal led to his execution."

There was a long silence. "Judas! Is that really you?" he asked uncertainly.

Isaac paused again for a brief second. "Yes, yes, Father, it is, but that wasn't the response I was expecting from you. I figured you would call me crazy and ask me to leave."

"The responsibility of that betrayal was not yours to bear alone Judas," he said plainly.

"How do you figure that, Father?"

"We met a long time ago. I was there, 2000 years ago. I am the one that handed down his sentence. I ordered his crucifixion. Judas, I'm Pontius Pilate."

Printed in Canada